PRELUDE TO LOVE

ANNE BARWELL

LACEDRAGON
PUBLISHING

Published by LaceDragon Publishing

All trademarks, brands, and or licensed materials mentioned are registered trademarks of their respective holders/companies.

Cover design: © 2019 Designs by Morningstar
https://morningstarashley.com/
Publishing logo © 2019 T.L. Bland
http://www.thruterryseyes.com/
Cover art is for illustrative purposes only and any person depicted on the cover is a model

Editing: Loretta Sylvestre

ISBN: 978-0-9951466-6-2 (epub)
ISBN: 978-0-9951466-7-9 (mobi)
ISBN: 978-0-9951466-8-6 (print)

First Edition published by Dreamspinner Press, 2018

AUTHOR'S NOTE:

Avalon College is fictional, although Avalon is a suburb of Lower Hutt. In New Zealand the terms high school and college are used interchangeably.

ALSO BY ANNE BARWELL

Slow Dreaming

On Wings of Song

The Sleepless City

Shades of Sepia

Electric Candle by Elizabeth Noble

Family and Reflection

Shifting Chaos by Elizabeth Noble

Echoes Rising

Shadowboxing

Winter Duet

Comes a Horseman

CO-WRITTEN WITH LOU SYLVRE

New Zealand Romance

Sunset at Pencarrow

Magic in the Isles

The Harp and the Sea

To all the musicians I've had the privilege of performing with.

ACKNOWLEDGMENTS

To Naomi, Belinda, Emma, Jax, Angela, and JJ for beta reading.

To my writing and reading communities for your support and friendship, in particular RWNZ, and my Facebook groups Anne's Books and Brews, Kiwi Authors Rainbow Readers, and Rainbow Readers Club. A special thanks to the New Zealand Rainbow Romance Writers group—you guys rock.

Gillian, Emma, and JJ for all their support, friendship, and awesome accountability.

Morningstar Ashley for her wonderful cover art.

Loretta for editing.

To my family. Love you.

CHAPTER ONE

Joel Ashcroft cringed when his student played yet another wrong note. He pointed with his pencil at the key signature of the music propped up on the piano.

"What key is that, Caleb?"

"G major, Mr Ashcroft."

"And that means?" Joel prompted when Caleb didn't elaborate further.

"Umm…" Caleb turned to Joel. "I don't remember." He thought for a moment. "It means all the notes are sharp, doesn't it? I'm sorry. I forgot! That's why it doesn't sound right."

Joel bit down on his lower lip and slowly counted to five before replying. "You're almost right, but not quite. Would you like to try again?"

How had this kid passed his grade one theory exam with honours? He'd forgotten everything he'd supposedly learnt the moment the exam finished.

"Oh right!" Caleb exclaimed. "It means all the Fs are sharp, doesn't it?"

Joel gripped his pencil tightly, half expecting it to snap in two. The universe was shitting on him by giving him these pupils last thing on a Friday afternoon. One day he'd rearrange his schedule so he didn't come home at the end of a week's work at the high school to spend another couple of hours teaching. A couple of weeks into the new school year and he was already feeling the strain.

"That's right. Well done." Joel forced a smile.

Caleb beamed at him and then began to play again, totally ignoring the conversation they'd just had.

Luckily, a knock at the door provided a brief escape. "Good evening, Mrs Barker," Joel said politely as he let her in. An attempt to block out the dissonant notes still coming from the other room failed miserably. "Please come in. We're nearly finished."

"Oh." Mrs Barker glanced at her watch. "I was just about to apologise for being early. Haven't you got another ten minutes to go?"

"We're finishing a little earlier tonight," Joel said firmly. "We had a longer lesson last week to make up the time."

"Oh, yes, so you did." Mrs Barker smiled at him, conveniently forgetting the previous week's lesson had been longer than usual because she'd been so late picking up her son. "I'm so proud of him, you know." She lowered her voice, although it was doubtful Caleb would hear, given how focused he was on his music.

Joel wished *he* could focus on something else.

Usually he had a lot more patience with Caleb, and the kid did try really hard. It wasn't Caleb's fault his mother had pushed him into learning an instrument he had no interest in.

"Yes, I know." Joel had tried once before to explain to this doting parent that Caleb loved the stage more than he did music, but she stubbornly refused to listen. "I heard the local theatre group is auditioning for a new play. Caleb was brilliant when he performed in the school production last year. Perhaps if he had the opportunity to—"

"My Caleb isn't going to be an actor." Mrs Barker gave Joel a glare. "He's a musician."

Joel sighed. Caleb had confided in him that he'd like to take a break from music until he'd had the chance to see if he wanted to further pursue acting. "Perhaps just think about it, hmm? He could always come back to music if it doesn't work out and pick up where he left off."

As if on cue, Caleb started to play the G major scale in the middle of the piece. Joel winced as the scale went through a couple of keys the composer hadn't intended.

"There's nothing to think about." Mrs Barker pushed past him into the music room. A huge smile lit up her face when she saw her son seated at the piano.

"Your mum's here," Joel said. "I'll see you next week, Caleb."

Caleb packed up his music while Joel scribbled a few notes about the day's lesson in his notebook. His friend Darin had once told him it was a good thing no one else could read his writing, given some of the comments he made.

"Thanks for the lesson, Mr Ashcroft," Caleb said politely. "See you next week."

"See you next week, Joel," Mrs Barker said as though their brief conversation had never taken place. "If you'd like to meet anytime to discuss his progress, you know I'm more than happy to, right?" She winked at him.

Joel bit his lip before replying. "Have a good week, Mrs Barker."

"Adelaide, please," Mrs Barker insisted. "After all, we've known each other a while now."

"Umm, yes, we have, but—"

"Just about done for today, Joel?" Darin Prior poked his head around the door. "Hi, Adelaide, how's it going?"

"I was just leaving." Adelaide Barker gave Darin an annoyed look. "I'll see *you* later," she told Joel and then hurried her son out the front door.

"I didn't hear you come in," Joel mumbled, slamming the cover shut on his notebook.

"I'm honing my ninja skills." Darin grinned.

"And you have a front door key," Joel added. When he'd struggled to get out of bed to answer the door the year before because of a bad case of flu, Darin and his wife, Ella, had decided someone needed to be able to get into the house in case of an emergency.

"Well, yeah, that too." Darin shook his head. "One of these days you'll have to tell her, you know. That woman's been flirting with you ever since you started working at the high school."

"Yeah, and if I tell her I'm gay, I might as well take out an ad in the paper and proclaim it to the whole region." Joel wasn't exactly in the closet, but he didn't make a point of discussing his sexuality. Not when he didn't have a reason to. He'd discovered the hard way that some stuff was better kept private.

"Not everyone is going to react like your dad did," Darin said quietly.

"I know that, but if I'm going to tell people, I'll be the one to tell them, not some woman who's trying to flirt with me." Joel made a point of bending to pick up his cat, Nannerl, when she rubbed up against him. Adelaide didn't mean any harm, and she was lonely since her husband died, but she wasn't Joel's type. He probably should have stopped her months ago, but it never seemed the right time. And he'd never been in the right headspace for what would come afterwards.

"You're hungry, aren't you, kitty?" Joel scratched behind

Nannerl's ears. "Don't worry, it's safe to come in again. The horrible noise is gone for another week."

"Maybe it's about time you started dating again," Darin suggested. He stroked Nannerl's fur, and the cat purred. "It's been five years since you broke up with Reed. He's moved on. You should too."

"Maybe I haven't met the right guy yet." Joel handed the cat to Darin and closed the piano lid. If he didn't close it now, he'd forget later, and Nannerl loved walking across the keys, preferably in the middle of the night. Not only that, but she was shedding like crazy, and he didn't want to find large piles of ginger fur on the keyboard in the morning. Some of it always managed to slide between the keys and it was a bitch to get out.

"You said that the last time we had this conversation." Darin carried Nannerl out to the kitchen, and Joel heard the fridge open.

"You'll need to open a new tin," he called out. He and Darin had flatted together in university days, while Joel was at uni and Darin did his apprenticeship. Once their studies were complete, they'd each settled down with the person they wanted to spend the rest of their lives with.

Darin and Ella were still together, but Joel had missed out on his own happy ending. When Reed got a job offer in Australia, Joel decided not to go with him. Wellington was his home, and he didn't want to leave behind the friends he considered family.

"Got it, thanks."

By the time Joel reached the kitchen, Darin had fed Nannerl and helped himself to a cup of coffee like he always did while he waited for Joel to tidy up after he'd finished teaching. Joel made extra coffee on Fridays for that reason. He and Darin usually went to the pub for an hour and then ended up at Darin's for dinner with his family. Most of the traditions they'd had when flatting hadn't survived, but that one had, and Joel looked forward to Friday evening each week. Ella was a good cook, and she and Joel had always got on well.

She'd appreciated that he'd suggested the no-brainer idea of moving out to live with Reed as soon as he'd finished his degree. Ella and Darin were madly in love, and Joel didn't want to intrude. She stayed over most nights anyway, so it made more sense for her to move in. Flatting with Reed had been more expensive, but Joel still managed to save enough to buy a place of his own. Luckily, he'd found his two-bedroom town house before prices had gone through the roof, so his repayments were cheaper than renting. He and Reed had discussed buying it together, but Reed hadn't been so sure. Maybe he'd had an inkling even then that their relationship wouldn't last. Joel preferred not to think about it too much.

Joel missed sharing his house. He had friends—Darin mostly—but it wasn't the same. Some nights it would be nice to curl up with someone who didn't shed fur all over him like Nannerl. And while Ella didn't begrudge the time Joel and Darin spent together, Darin's focus needed to be on his family. Joel might be honorary uncle to Darin's daughter, Isabel, but he wasn't family.

"Ella heard from Marcus earlier in the week." Darin gave Joel a look. "You're listening to me, right? You've got that miles-away look you do so well." He rolled his eyes. "Musicians."

Joel snorted. "Mechanics," he countered. "I've seen that look on your face too, and nine times out of ten you're thinking about Ella."

"So? I figure nine times out of ten, you're thinking about some hot guy. No difference."

"Whatever."

"Whatever." Darin leaned over and poked Joel in the shoulder. "So, as I was saying. Marcus. You remember Marcus, right?"

"Yeah, I remember Marcus." Joel focused on finding a clean plastic lid for the new tin of cat food. "Ella's brother, right?"

They'd first met at Ella and Darin's wedding fourteen years before. Joel had been best man and Ella had persuaded Marcus—who preferred to stay out of the lime-light—to take on the role of usher. It had been Joel's one and only trip to Hokitika. Reed had stayed behind, as they'd been going through a rough patch at the time, but Joel had nevertheless enjoyed his visit to the west coast of the South Island.

"Right." Darin grew quiet, something that didn't happen often.

Joel stopped what he was doing and gave him a suspicious look. "And?" He swore he could see tiny clockworks going around in Darin's brain. Subtlety had never been one of his friend's strong points.

Yeah, he remembered Marcus. The guy was tall, ripped, and had amazing grey eyes. Joel had taken one look at him, and the witty comment he'd been about to say had disappeared, leaving him tongue-tied and mumbling. Then, to add insult to injury, Marcus had shaken Joel's hand and introduced him to the man standing next him—his boyfriend.

Joel had been mortified by his reaction, as he and Marcus were both spoken for. He'd turned instinctively to apologise to Reed and introduce him, only to remember he wasn't there.

He'd felt like an idiot. Meeting again at the Prior's Friday night dinners during Marcus's infrequent visits to Wellington hadn't been much better. Joel had swung between awkward silence and talking nonstop. Marcus was seriously hot, but Joel wasn't about to pursue a guy who was already in a relationship.

"And?" Darin seemed amused. "Oh, yeah. Marcus is moving up here from Hokitika permanently and will be living with us till he finds a place of his own. So you'll see him again next Friday, if not before."

Joel slammed the fridge shut. "That will be nice," he mumbled. A couple of years had passed since their last meeting, so hopefully this time Joel's hormones would be better behaved. "Is his boyfriend moving up here with him?"

"Oh, didn't I mention that?" Darin opened the back door to let the cat out. "He's single, has been for about six months."

Marcus Verden switched on his mobile as soon as he exited the plane. No messages, except one from his ex-boyfriend, Garth. Marcus sighed and deleted the text without reading it. Although Garth had agreed it was time to end their relationship, he persisted in texting Marcus—far too often. Marcus had moved on. It was time Garth did too.

The landing had been bumpy, but the woman next to him had assured him that was normal for Wellington. Gale force winds were common, even during summer, and they had to be a lot worse than this before anyone worried about them. She'd be more concerned if the air was still. Earthquake weather and all that.

Marcus had nodded politely. He wasn't fond of flying, but Ella had convinced him to book a flight instead of taking a bus then catching the ferry. It hadn't taken much to persuade him. His stomach loved Cook Strait even less than it did air turbulence, and he'd sold his SUV as part of his business. He'd find a new vehicle as soon as he was settled.

"Uncle Marcus!" Isabel waved frantically from behind the arrival gate. He waved back and sprinted over to her.

"You've grown, Issy." Marcus gave her a hug.

He took a step back to get a better look. When he'd seen her last, she'd been a little girl. Now she looked more like a young lady. Her long hair, previously worn in two plaits, was free of its restraints and almost down to her waist. She definitely took after the Prior side of the family, with auburn hair like her father's and his often-weird sense of humour. Her grey eyes reminded Marcus of Grandma Verden's, though, as did her smile; Marcus had been told he had it too.

People always saw who they wanted to in others, he figured.

"Growth spurt." Darin held out his hand. They shook hands and then embraced briefly.

Darin was a good guy, and he'd always taken care of Ella and Isabel. He and Marcus didn't see each other often, but when they did, they picked up where they'd left off as though no time had passed at all.

Given the difference in Isabel, however, it was obviously longer since they'd seen each other than Marcus realised. He quickly did the maths—she'd be fourteen in a couple of months. How could he have forgotten? He sent her birthday presents every April, and Ella and her family had made frequent trips to the South Island. That had stopped when Marcus and Ella's parents had retired. They wanted to see more of New Zealand, so they travelled, which meant they were rarely available for visits.

When Marcus was invited to come to Wellington to visit, he'd declined. He used his dislike of travel as an excuse and told himself he needed to spend more time with Garth. They both worked and time together was precious. But then, the last time… He'd chosen Garth over family, and he'd ended up alone.

Walking through the airport with Isabel and Darin, Marcus felt a pang of guilt. Family was important, and Ella was his only sibling. It wouldn't have hurt him to make the trip to Wellington more often. After he couldn't use Garth as a pretext, he'd tired himself out with his job in an attempt to forget his ex.

Isabel hooked her arm through Marcus's. "Come on. We need to pick up your bags from the luggage area before it gets really busy."

Darin laughed. "Remind you of anyone?"

"Oh, yes." Marcus ignored Isabel's scowl. "Just like her mum at that age."

"Only at that age?" Darin put on a hangdog expression Marcus didn't buy for an instant. "See what I have to put up with? It will be great to have another guy in the house for a while."

"Uh-huh." Marcus could read between the lines. Someone to run interference and commiserate with, although it was obvious Darin enjoyed every minute of it. He loved his girls, and it showed.

"I'm here, and I can hear you, you know." Isabel gave a dramatic sigh and tossed her hair back over her shoulders, yet the twinkle in her eyes belied the action.

"Of course you can." Darin rolled his eyes and ruffled his daughter's hair, which earned him an identical reaction.

Marcus chuckled. The two of them made a great double act. He was in for an interesting few months until he found a place of his own. Definitely the distraction he needed.

He glanced at them and caught their twin looks of concern, although they both hid their expressions quickly. How much had Ella told them?

Luckily, his suitcase was one of the first through the conveyor belt, and it wasn't long before they were driving on the Hutt Valley motorway, heading to Petone—and to what was now home.

Marcus leaned back in his seat, ignoring the chatter between Isabel and her father. He stared out at the harbour, watching the waves crash against the shore and letting his mind wander. He'd done the right thing relocating here, hadn't he?

He loved Hokitika and had lived there all his life, but like all smaller towns, everyone knew everyone else's business. Not only that; it was impossible to avoid Garth. Marcus's face had flamed several times at the whispers and sympathetic looks. The locals didn't judge and continued to be as friendly as they always had, but in a way that was worse. He'd never move forward with his life until he lived somewhere no one knew him and he could avoid reminders of his life with Garth.

Ella had suggested the move to Wellington. Brendan, a friend of a friend, planned to retire from his lawn mowing business within the next couple of years, and he would be more than happy to take on someone now who could eventually take over. Marcus had provided the service in his home town for years and had no problems getting the references he needed. He'd also built up his business to include gardening, odd jobs, and the like. He'd spoken to Brendan on the phone a few times, and the older man sounded keen about the idea of diversifying. With the weather derailing his lawn mowing jobs several days at a time throughout the year, it would give the business a steadier income. While Wellington had a mild climate compared to other parts of the country, it also had a tendency to rain a lot, and not only in winter.

"Another ten minutes and we'll be home." Darin moved into the left lane and exited the motorway. "We've done a bit of decorating since you were here last. Ella's in a decluttering mood, so watch where you put anything; it will disappear before you can blink. She's been reading that book." He turned to Isabel. "What was it called again?"

"*Spark Joy*. It's about tidying up. I think it's great."

"I've already told her she's not allowed near my garage," Darin muttered. He cleared his throat. "Yeah, it's great."

Marcus was impressed by the way Darin managed to make his comment sound almost sincere.

"I haven't heard of it." Marcus had the latest Lee Child novel in his carry-on. He'd planned to read it on the way to distract himself from the trip, but by the time the air hostess had served tea and Anzac biscuits, it wasn't long before preparations were being made to land. "Probably not my thing anyway."

About ten minutes later, Darin pulled up the driveway of the Prior's older, bungalow-style house.

"You've cleaned up the garden, and the lawns look great." Marcus always noticed that about a house first. A side effect of his job.

The backyard was much bigger than he remembered, but the last time he'd visited, the front of the house had been overgrown, with a random selection of shrubbery and an overwhelming smell of lavender.

Roses adorned one side of the driveway, a mix of miniature and climbing along the fence line in multiple colours. The lawns were neatly mowed, and there wasn't a weed in sight.

"It's taken all our time to get this part of the section looking good." Darin opened the boot to retrieve Marcus's suitcase, but Marcus grabbed it first. "The back still looks like a jungle."

"I'd like to help you with that, if that's okay," Marcus said.

"I was hoping you'd say that!" Ella came up behind them.

Marcus turned and pulled his sister into an embrace.

"Ella! It's good to see you." They'd always been close, as there was only a year between them in age.

"Let me look at you, baby brother." Ella looked smug when Marcus's face crinkled up into an expression of disgust.

"Less of the baby, big sister," he muttered. "You're looking good, Ella."

Ella nodded, distracted. "Hmm. You've lost weight, and you have bags under your eyes. We'll have to do something about that."

"You've given me a place to stay until I find somewhere of my own," Marcus protested, as much for his own protection than anything else. He knew that look in her eye. She already had a plan in place. He glanced around, ready to ask Darin for support, but he and Isabel had conveniently disappeared into the house.

"That's what families do." Ella lowered her voice. "Don't worry, I haven't told them too much. None of the details, just that you've come up here for a fresh start. We're here for you. You're not alone in this."

"I know, and thanks."

His parents had been supportive too, but they'd always liked Garth, so Marcus didn't want to sour the relationship they had with him. The dairy farm Garth worked with his brother had been in the Kenway family for two generations, so he wasn't leaving the area anytime soon. Marcus decided it made sense for him to be the one to move away—he couldn't expect Garth to give up everything he and his family had built while Marcus could do what he loved anywhere.

Except be with the person he'd once loved and who he'd once thought loved him back.

To make matters worse, Garth seemed keen to continue to be in Marcus's life, if not as a lover, then as a friend. He'd told Garth he needed to put some distance between them first, but Garth didn't seem to understand. Marcus had tried to explain, but he sucked at that kind of thing. It was easier to put it all behind him and ignore Garth's attempts to contact him. At least for now.

"You're thinking about it again." Ella ushered him inside. "*I'm* thinking a bit of distraction is exactly what you need."

Darin met them at the door. "I'll get Marcus settled," he suggested. "I've checked dinner, and it has about another ten minutes to go, so I've put the kettle on. Marcus, you still as addicted to coffee as ever?"

"Some things never change." Marcus sniffed the air. "Hmm, that chilli smells wonderful. Anything I can do to help?"

"Don't worry. You're going to earn your keep getting my garden into shape. The back section's so big I can't keep up with it." Ella winked at him, although he knew she was only teasing. He fully intended to help out where he could, and her garden would be the perfect thing to keep busy with.

"I'll show you to your room, Uncle Marcus, and then Dad can show you around. I'm learning piano now." Isabel led Marcus down the hallway, barely catching her breath before continuing. "I really love it, and Uncle Joel's a good teacher."

"Joel? As in your dad's best man?" Marcus asked. The weekend of Darin and Ella's wedding had been a bit of a blur, and he'd got very drunk on the night they'd said their vows. Darin and Joel had been friends for years… or something like that. Cute guy, but Marcus hadn't paid him much attention after Garth had first inserted himself into the conversation, and then cut it off as soon as it had begun. Marcus had enjoyed seeing Joel now and then at family dinners, and he'd upgraded his assessment from 'cute' to 'hot.' After that, he'd taken an emotional step back, reminding himself that he loved Garth and their relationship was important to him.

"Yes, that's right. He still comes around for dinner every

Friday, so you'll meet him again soon anyway." Isabel opened the door at the end of the hallway, letting Marcus peer inside. "Or maybe even sooner if you'd take me to my lesson tomorrow night. Mum's got some work to do for a PTA meeting, and Dad has a job he needs to finish, so he'll be working late."

"Hmm." Marcus took in the room Isabel showed him. It would be his for a good few months. Before he committed himself to finding a home, he wanted to be very sure he'd made the right decision moving up here and that this new business would work out.

The last time he'd visited, this had been Ella's sewing and craft room, with piles of material layered on top of one another and a sewing machine in the corner. Pink rainbows and unicorns had adorned the walls, left over from the previous owners of the house, who had used it as a nursery.

Now it was tastefully decorated with cream-painted walls and a couple of canvas prints of what he presumed were local scenery. He looked closer and recognised the view of the harbour and the Settlers Museum. The room felt very peaceful, and he sighed aloud and nodded. He put his bag down in the corner next to the bed. He could imagine himself here. This would do nicely.

"Oh, good," Isabel said. "That's settled, then. Thanks. I knew you'd say yes!"

"Uh, what?" Marcus hadn't agreed to anything.

Isabel smiled at him, and he knew he'd totally missed something. "I'd better practise tonight. After all, I'd be terribly embarrassed if I didn't play well at my lesson tomorrow, as you're going to be there." She hugged him tightly. "Thanks, Uncle Marcus!"

Marcus scratched his head as he watched her go, unsure whether he should be amused or terrified by how easily she'd played him. A little too much like her mother, that was for sure.

He shrugged and headed to the kitchen and the welcome smell of coffee. It wouldn't do any harm to take his niece to her music lesson. With everything she and her parents were doing for him, it was the least he could do.

CHAPTER TWO

"Turn left here," Isabel said, "and then right into that grove there. Uncle Joel lives almost at the end of the street on the left."

Marcus followed Isabel's directions and pulled up in front of the one-storey duplex she'd indicated. Grey-and-white birds cooed outside, busying themselves finding food in the grass under the large pōhutukawa trees lining the street. Despite it being mid-February, the distinctive spray-like red blooms usually associated with Christmas still covered many of them. The house looked tidy and well cared for, although the lawn needed a trim.

By the time Marcus got out of the car, Isabel had already walked up the short path to the front door. She waited until Marcus caught up and then knocked.

The man who answered was a fraction taller than Marcus's six foot. He had dark hair cut short at the sides and left to grow long on top so his fringe flopped forward on one side. Marcus took a step closer to introduce himself and stared into striking blue eyes.

Wow. Joel was everything he remembered, and more.

"I don't know if you remember me." Marcus's voice came out hoarser than he intended. "I'm Marcus, Isabel's uncle. Her parents are busy, so you're stuck with me today. It's nice to see you again. It's been a couple of years at least."

"Nice to see you again, too." Joel shook Marcus's hand with a firm grip, although his palm felt a little damp. "Come on in. The lesson before Isabel's cancelled, so we can get started straight away."

"Thanks." Marcus let go of Joel's hand and moved aside to let Isabel enter the house first.

"Darin told me you'd moved up this way." Joel followed Isabel down the hallway to what Marcus presumed must be the music room. "Wellington's not bad once you get used to the wind, or so I've been told. I've always lived here."

Joel paused as though coming up for air. Marcus opened his mouth to remind him he'd experienced Wellington's weather before, but before he could, Joel continued speaking.

"There's a sofa in the music room for parents to sit on. I won't be a moment, need to refill my water. Do you want any?"

"No, I'm fine, thanks."

"Okay." Joel disappeared through the doorway at the opposite side of the hallway.

Isabel grinned and settled herself on the piano stool. "Wow. I don't think I've ever heard Uncle Joel talk that much and so fast." She retrieved her music from her bag and placed it on the piano. "I think you guys are going to get on really, really well."

"Is that right?" Marcus murmured, but if Isabel heard him, she chose not to reply.

Instead she began playing, a succession of notes up and down the piano, first with one hand, and then the other, picking up speed as she went.

"You've been practising your scales, I see." Joel gave

Marcus a nod before sitting down on the chair next to the piano. He seemed a little calmer than before he'd left the room, although still nervous about something. "As you've already played your scales, could you play me the exercise I set you last week?" Joel scribbled something in a notebook on the table next to the piano. "Do you have your theory book? I'll mark it while I listen."

Isabel handed Joel a book and then began to play.

Marcus tapped his foot along with the music. He'd always enjoyed listening to music, despite knowing next to nothing about the technical side of it. He vaguely remembered learning how to read music when he was at school, although he'd never paid much attention to the lessons.

"Very good. You've definitely been practising a lot this week. You've got the hang of the new time signature in your theory too." Joel leaned over, still holding a pencil. "There's one thing with the grouping of the notes you haven't got quite right, though."

Isabel looked at whatever he showed her and nodded. "Oh, I see what I did. I forgot it's compound time, so the notes need to be grouped in threes, not twos."

"That's right." Joel smiled, the side of his mouth crinkling. Although the comment wasn't directed at him, Marcus smiled in return. "Now let's look at the next page in the book. It's back to the circle of keys this week."

Marcus listened for a moment but zoned out as soon as Joel began talking about enharmonic equivalents—whatever that meant. Joel moved in closer to Isabel as he spoke so they could both see the book. He spoke slowly enough to ensure she could follow what he was saying, and he was careful to pause in places to give her the opportunity to ask questions. He must have taught the subject many times before, yet he still sounded enthusiastic. Although Marcus had given up trying to understand what Joel was talking about, the timbre of his voice was relaxing. Marcus leaned back on the sofa and closed his eyes, tired after the upheaval of the past few days.

He opened his eyes with a start when Joel stopped talking, and immediately felt bad that he'd felt relaxed enough to drift off. He was supposed to be listening to the lesson and Isabel's playing. After all, that was the reason she'd asked him to bring her, right?

Isabel stood to pack her bag. She turned to Joel, frowning. "Shouldn't your next pupil be here by now?"

"Joseph's coming on Fridays now. He's playing water polo on Tuesdays, so his mum asked if he could swap days." Joel shrugged. "I was happy to change things around for him. Tonight is my lesson prep night, so it gives me more time for that."

"Darin said you teach at the local high school too?" Marcus wanted to know more about Joel. Surely he wasn't making ends meet by teaching a few kids after school? He wracked his memory but couldn't remember if that had come up in conversation during those family dinners. Even if it had, Joel's situation could have changed since then.

A large ginger cat wandered into the room and made a beeline for Isabel. She bent to pat the cat, which started purring loudly. "Can I take Nannerl out to the kitchen and give her some treats?"

"Sure." Joel rolled his eyes. "I swear that cat loves you and your dad more than she loves me. As soon as either of you are here, it's as though I don't exist. Treats are in the usual place, but don't give her too many even if she begs for them."

"I won't." Isabel left the room, the cat following closely behind.

"Nannerl?" Marcus asked. It seemed a strange name for a cat—unless he was missing something.

"She's a girl, so I couldn't call her Wolfgang." Joel spoke like the comment explained everything.

"Huh?"

"Wolfgang," Joel repeated. "Amadeus Mozart," he added when Marcus still looked none the wiser.

"Oh." Marcus couldn't think of anything to say that wouldn't sound as unenlightened as he felt.

"Nannerl was Mozart's sister." Joel frowned. "You're not into music, are you?"

"Not into classical music," Marcus corrected. "I like music as much as the next guy. I'm just not as clued up on it as you are. There's not much call for that stuff in my line of work."

"Oh, right. Yes." Joel paused as though frantically trying to remember what Marcus did for a living.

"I mow lawns and do a bit of gardening and odd jobs. Had my own business in Hokitika, but I'm starting work with someone else up here. At least for now. It depends how everything pans out." Marcus wasn't sure why he'd gone into so much detail. All he'd planned to say was that he mowed lawns. His hopes for the future were his own business, and it wasn't as though a guy he'd only met a few times would be interested.

"Ah yes. I remember now." Joel screwed up his nose. "I probably should apologise for the state of my section, then. I don't get the chance to mow very often, with all the time I spend at school and then a couple of afternoons teaching here too. I spend one day of my weekend on school stuff, and then it tends to rain on the other."

"I could mow your lawns for you," Marcus offered before he realised what he was doing.

Joel looked mortified. "I couldn't ask you to do that!" His eyes glazed over for a moment before he flushed bright red. "You'd… I mean…" He took a deep breath. "I'd pay you of course."

"If you want to, but it's not necessary." Marcus hadn't intended to ask for money at all. Joel was a friend of Darin's, and Isabel obviously doted on him. He'd been going to do it as a favour for his brother-in-law, but if Joel felt happier paying him, he wasn't going to argue the point. "You seemed busy, and I figured I could help. I'm not trying to drum up business."

He wasn't sure what Brendan would think of him taking on new customers without discussing it first, but this was something he could do on his weekend. And that way Joel would be around too, and they could...

Marcus swallowed. What the hell was he doing? He wasn't in the habit of using his lawn mowing to pick up men. Especially men who were best friends with members of his family, and sexy as hell to boot.

He wasn't in the habit of picking up men, period. He'd come to Wellington for a fresh start, not another relationship. Still, it couldn't hurt to make new friends, right? That was what people did, and if he was going to see Joel at family dinners, it would be easier if they were on friendly terms. They'd never really got to know each other when Marcus had visited Wellington before. A few conversations over dinner didn't count.

"I didn't think you were—and thanks."

Isabel came back into the room, the cat trailing behind her. Nannerl purred loudly and brushed herself against Marcus's legs. He bent to pat her without thinking. "Oh, look, Uncle Joel, Nannerl likes him!" She handed Marcus a glass of water. "It's quite hot in here, isn't it? I thought you might like some water."

Joel glanced at Isabel and then Nannerl. "That cat is usually very standoffish. Did you sneak some cat treats into Marcus's pocket, Issy?"

Isabel grinned, though Marcus didn't believe her innocent look for even a moment. Her expression reminded him too much of her mother's. "Of course not! Nannerl's just made a new friend. Haven't you, kitty?"

Joel stretched his shoulders and leaned back in his chair. The day had been a busy one, and transposing the music for that week's choir practice had taken longer than he'd anticipated. Leaving it in its original key would have been easier for him but not for the kids who had struggled with the high notes the week before. Unfortunately the school's budget was already stretched thin so asking them to spend money on transposition software wasn't an option. He ran his fingers through his hair and glanced at the clock on the classroom wall. Crap. He'd worked past dinnertime again.

Closing his eyes, he let his mind drift back to the previous evening. Despite behaving like a complete idiot when Marcus had arrived, he figured he'd salvaged the situation reasonably well once he'd forced himself to calm down.

Joel took pride in keeping his cool in most situations, but for some reason when he met Marcus, he'd reacted like a hormonal teenager. He hadn't babbled like that in years—a leftover habit from his childhood put behind him long ago— or at least since the last time he'd seen Marcus. And then when Marcus had offered to mow his lawns, Joel had immediately visualised a shirtless Marcus, abs dripping with perspiration.

He glanced around the classroom. It looked tidy enough —Diane and Tina had done a good job cleaning up, although he'd told them to leave the whiteboard as he hadn't quite finished with it. Still hadn't quite finished with it.

Where was his notepad? He hunted through his desk and

finally found it underneath the empty cup from that morning's coffee.

"I figured you'd still be here."

"Hi, Ella." Joel began looking for his pen. He'd had it a few moments before. "You here for the PTA meeting?"

Ella handed him his pen. "Yes, unfortunately." She'd joined the Parent Teacher Association earlier that year after Isabel had started high school at Avalon College.

"Unfortunately?" Joel raised one eyebrow. "Thanks for the pen. Where was it?"

"On the floor in front of your desk. It rolled off when you shifted your cup." Ella walked around to his side of the desk. "Adelaide Barker's on the warpath. She's got some fundraising ideas I thought you might want a heads up about." She paused. "I'd like your input before I go for or against whatever she puts forward."

"Yes?" Joel stood and offered Ella his seat, then pulled across a stool and perched on it. "This has the sound of something I'm not going to like."

"That depends," Ella said cautiously. "I think the idea has some merit, so I'd like to be able to support her, but it is going to be a lot of work for you if the board agrees to go along with it, so I wanted to run it past you first to see if it's feasible."

"I'm listening."

"Adelaide thinks—and I agree—that the school choir and orchestra sounded really good at prize-giving at the end of last year. You've done amazing work with those kids, and it's obvious they're enjoying it too."

"Thanks. I'm proud of them. They've worked hard and it shows."

The orchestra and choir were Joel's pet projects. When he'd arrived at the school, there hadn't been much in the way of opportunity for music performance. His predecessor had a choir of sorts who were taught by an itinerant music teacher who came in once a week, and the kids had to audition in order to take part. Most of the students involved attended under protest because their parents had pushed them into it. Although their teacher had done what he could, the choir had quickly disbanded when he'd left.

"Adelaide's idea is to put on a concert so the kids can show off what they can do." Ella paused. "You probably know that we're losing some of our funding, but it's not common knowledge yet how much that's going to impact. It's one of the items on the agenda for this evening's meeting."

"How bad is it?" Joel's department relied on the generous donations for a lot more than buying new equipment. Fund raising such as sausage sizzles and cake stalls only brought in so much, and many of their parents were struggling financially too.

"Don Lester is retiring, and the new owner of his firm isn't as community minded."

"But he—"

"Exactly."

"Shit." Joel bit his lip. "We can't run the itinerant teaching programme without that money, and most of our kids can't afford to learn privately. Their instrument hire is part of that too. We can't let that happen." Not only did it give the kids the opportunity to learn music, but it kept many of them busy outside school hours, and out of trouble. "Doesn't this new guy realise the impact of his decision?"

"Some of that decision is financial too. Perhaps in a few years when he's settled into his new business and can be confident it's running at a profit..." Ella shook her head. "I might not agree with his decision, but we need to respect it. Even if he does change his mind, we still need to find enough to cover the shortfall for at least the second half of the year."

"That soon?"

"Yeah. So the concert needs to be sooner rather than later. Any idea of a feasible timeline? If I can go to the board with that tonight, it would support Adelaide's idea, and get the ball rolling."

"I'm not going to push the kids into something they don't want to do, especially as it would mean extra rehearsals, but I don't think that will be a problem once they find out what we're fundraising for. The parents will help out as well." Joel made a mental note to thank Adelaide for her support to keep his department afloat. While she could be a little full on at times, she had a good heart, and a generous nature. "We could aim for May, as that would give us a couple of months' rehearsals. We also have some new kids this year, and we don't want to scare them off." Joel chewed on the end of his pencil. If they didn't pull this off, that would be a moot point anyway. Most of his orchestra would lose their instruments and their teachers, and there wouldn't be enough kids to keep it going. "Perhaps a couple of pieces each, and for the finale the orchestra can accompany the choir?" He sucked on the end of his pencil. "Do you want me to come to the meeting with you?"

His stomach rumbled, a reminder he hadn't had dinner yet. He'd grab something later if Ella wanted him there. This idea had a lot going for it, but he'd have to ensure it didn't expand into something totally unrealistic.

"You need to go home and eat." Ella got up from the desk. "I've got this, but I wanted your input first. So, a short concert, about half an hour to an hour long? Hmm, have you —never mind."

"Never mind what?" Joel knew that look. Ella wouldn't have mentioned anything unintentionally.

"How long has it been since you performed in public?" Ella asked a question she already knew the answer to.

"I'm not doing that." Joel's stomach churned at the

memory of the concert he'd hung all his dreams on. Instead of being the beginning of a wonderful career in performance, it had brought his planned future crumbling down around him, and he'd vowed to put the whole embarrassing incident behind him. Even the memory of it made him sick to his stomach. "Not again. Not ever."

"You accompany the choir all the time. I've heard you play solo since that evening. You're still a brilliant pianist."

"There's a huge difference between playing at home for friends or in front of a hall full of kids, and a public performance." Joel failed to hide the bitterness in his voice.

"Think about it, hmm?" Ella headed for the door. "Don't worry, I won't mention it as an option during the meeting." She gave him a bright smile. "Just between you and me for the moment, okay?"

"Okay." Joel watched her go and sat staring for several minutes at the door she'd shut behind her.

He couldn't let the kids lose their access to music. He'd fight to make sure that didn't happen. Free time was a myth, right? He'd do whatever it took and worry about taking a break later.

No point in waiting until he'd asked his students whether they'd be interested to figure out what music they'd perform either. If he was going to sell this idea, he needed to have all his ducks in a row first and anticipate any questions they'd ask. Joel scribbled a few notes and threw his planner into his bag. As he felt around for his car keys, a note fell out, a reminder that he needed to buy milk on the way home.

Damn it. He'd forgotten about that. At this rate, he wouldn't have time to do a supermarket run until the weekend. It would be a good idea to stock up with everything he'd need on his way home. He could find something for dinner at the same time. Two birds. One stone.

By the time he'd driven around a few times to find a

parking spot at the supermarket he already had a short fuse. "Milk for coffee," he muttered. And if he didn't eat properly, he'd have Ella and Darin on his arse too. Ella always checked over Friday dinner that he was taking the time to look after himself. Sure, she tried to be subtle about it, but they both knew what she was doing.

Joel loved her for it anyway. Families looked after each other, or at least they were supposed to.

He grabbed his trolley and headed into the supermarket, a sale on chocolate catching his eye. Chocolate was made with vegetables, right? He could totally justify a couple of blocks. He paused, trying to decide between Black Forest and Caramel, threw both blocks into the trolley, and promptly hit another trolley with his, nearly sending an old lady sprawling.

"Oh my God, I'm so sorry." Joel helped her steady herself. "Totally my fault as I wasn't watching where I was going."

"It's fine." The lady straightened her hat and gave him a shaky smile which immediately turned down at the edge of her mouth. "Joel? It is Joel, yes? My you're grown since I saw you last."

Joel took a moment to place her. "Mrs Wakeman. It has been a while." No wonder she'd frowned. No doubt his father had said all manner of things to his secretary after Joel had moved out. Molly Wakeman had worked for Claude for years, and only taken retirement five years ago because her family had convinced her to.

She patted his arm. "You're holding up well. It's good to see you again. I was so sorry to hear about your father."

"That darn rain is settling in." Brendan peered outside and topped up both his and Marcus's coffees. "Wettest week we've had for a while. Everything's going to be too soggy to mow for the next few days."

"What do you usually do when you get days like this?" Marcus took another sip of coffee. Brendan was good to work for, and they got on well. They'd been using their down time to go over the plans Marcus had for the business and come up with a few extra ideas. He was glad Brendan was sticking around for a while before Marcus took over completely.

"I usually have a few inside jobs lined up, but they've been a bit lean of late." Brendan offered Marcus a gingernut, but he shook his head. "I've always run that side of the business on word of mouth, and haven't had to spend much on advertising, but there's more competition out there than there used to be." He shrugged. "Lawn mowing is up, though, with more people working and not having the time to do it themselves. Plenty of that to go around."

"Once it stops raining." Marcus's phone buzzed with a text. He ignored it.

"Should you get that?"

"No." Marcus's phone buzzed again. "For fuck's sake." He glanced at it in case it was important, but it was only another message from Garth. "Sorry."

"Girlfriend problems?"

"Ex-boyfriend." Marcus said, hoping it would stop Brendan asking any more questions. He wasn't getting back together with Garth, no matter how many times he texted, or rang. Marcus had skimmed the first couple of texts then deleted the rest. He hadn't listened to the voice messages as he wasn't sure he could be as strong while hearing Garth's voice. He'd loved that voice once, and the way Garth had said his name had always made him smile.

"Sounds like he hasn't got the message he's an ex yet." Brendan stirred a spoonful of sugar into his coffee. "Sometimes you have to rip the Band-Aid off in order to move forward."

"That's why I'm in Wellington." Marcus closed his eyes, not wanting to dwell on how things had gone so badly wrong between them. They'd been happy once, and then all their hopes and dreams had disappeared in a haze of apathy. He'd made the decision to end things, and although Garth had said he'd understood his actions showed he hadn't.

"Hmm." Brendan studied him for a moment. "Do you still love the guy?"

"No." Marcus's memories of their years together felt like watching someone else. Garth had wanted to be wherever Marcus was to the point of smothering him. Every time he planned anything, Garth had to be a part of it, isolating Marcus until he'd nearly lost all his friends. Those who remained had encouraged Marcus to forge his own way in life—and told him he should have done so sooner. Of course, in hindsight, now he had space to think, the situation he'd been in was much clearer, but he'd convinced himself for years that he needed to be a better boyfriend, and that what Garth wanted wasn't unreasonable.

"Tempted to give things another chance, though, yeah?"

"Definitely not." Marcus hadn't come all this way for a fresh start to be sucked back into a relationship with someone he had no feelings for.

"Good." Brendan nodded. "I've been with my Lucy for thirty years now, but I wasted a lot of time before that with the wrong person. All the signs were there but I ignored them, then after I broke it up, I didn't get close to anyone for a long time, because I thought the breakup had been some-thing I'd done. Nearly missed getting together with the love of my life because I was an idiot."

"We only split up six months ago." Marcus usually wouldn't feel the need to explain himself, but as Brendan had gone out on a limb and talked about something personal, Marcus owed him at least a one sentence reply.

Brendan tilted his head to one side. "I met Lucy a few months after I'd split from Nan, and I couldn't see what was in front of me. Nearly lost her because I was a pigheaded fool. Love hits you when and where you least expect it."

"I'll keep that in mind." Marcus paused. "Thanks."

"You do that." Brendan glanced out the window again. "Looks like that rain is clearing, so we might get some ground dug over if nothing else." He grinned. "I used to mow Lucy's lawns for free, you know."

"I was planning to do the first mow free for a friend this weekend." Marcus used Brendan's comment as a segue into something he needed to bring up anyway. "I'll be doing it outside business hours once the weather improves, so—"

"Totally fine." Brendan smiled. "It's your business too, Marcus, so you don't need to justify your time."

"He's a family friend," Marcus elaborated so Brendan didn't get the wrong idea.

"So was my Lucy. Sometimes friendship grows into other things, sometimes it doesn't, but as I said, you don't have to justify anything to me. At the end of the day, the only person who knows what's in your heart is yourself."

"What are you going to play at the concert, Mr Ashcroft?" Austin was already waiting in the classroom when Joel arrived the next morning.

"Play at the concert?" Joe frowned. He hadn't told the kids about the concert yet, let alone that he'd be playing. He'd told Ella he wouldn't be. A familiar knot formed in his stomach. He'd definitely told her no.

And spent most of the night unable to sleep because of it.

"I overheard my parents talking last night." Austin's dad was on the PTA. "I think a concert to save the music department is a great idea." His expression grew sombre. "We're not really going to lose everything, are we? I love playing trombone, and I don't want to give that up." He chewed on his bottom lip. "I don't want you to lose your job either. That won't happen, right?"

"I'm not losing my job," Joel reassured him. "And don't worry, I'll be doing whatever I can to make sure you don't have to give up your trombone either."

"Why would Austin have to give up his trombone?" Tina walked into the classroom, Diane close at her heels. Both girls played violin, and they were inseparable since they'd started at the school two years ago. They'd talked about studying music at university; their dreams reminded Joel of his own at that age.

Joel took a deep breath. So much for keeping the concert a secret. The school had a healthy grapevine, and although Austin shouldn't have been eavesdropping it was too late to put the cat back into the bag. "Unfortunately we're losing some funding," Joel explained, choosing his words carefully. "But the PTA has come up with a great idea to cover the shortfall. We're going to have a concert to raise money."

"Will that be enough?" Diane was the quieter of the two, and always asked the practical questions.

"I hope so." Joel wouldn't lie to his students, but he didn't want them to worry either. "I'm going to ask everyone in the orchestra and choir whether they want to take part. It's going to be a lot of work and—"

"Yes!" The three students chorused as one.

Austin grinned. "Everyone's going to want to do this, Mr Ashcroft. It will be fun, and then we know we've all done our bit, right?"

"Right." Joel smiled at their enthusiasm.

"I'm excited that you're going to play too," Tina said. "I think it will be great. Do you know what you're going to play?"

Joel sighed. He couldn't expect them to perform and then refuse to do it himself. What kind of example would that be? His bad experience had been a long time ago. He wasn't that person now. He could do this. He'd have to do this. "I haven't decided yet, but I'll make a decision soon. I'll have to do heaps of practise too."

CHAPTER THREE

"I thought the PTA meeting went well." Ella broke the awkward silence at the dinner table the following Friday. She passed the bowl of roast vegetable salad to Joel.

"I thought you weren't going to suggest I perform at the concert." Joel took the bowl, dished himself out a generous amount, and then handed it to Marcus, who was seated on his right. "I told you it wasn't going to happen."

Marcus decided to say nothing. Joel had been quiet when he'd arrived for dinner, and judging from the glances Ella and Darin kept exchanging, that wasn't normal. Hopefully they would be able to find out what was wrong. After all, they knew Joel better than he did.

"*I* didn't suggest it," Ella said. "Adelaide did, and then everyone else was all over it. One of the parents remembered you from high school and some concert you performed in back then."

"Of course she did, and that was before that other… thing," Joel muttered. "I got into school the next morning, and everyone was talking about something I hadn't even agreed to! Not only that, but the kids are all over it, so I couldn't tell them I couldn't do it. And if I back out now, I'll feel like a heel."

"That other... thing might have been a one off," Darin said.

"But what if it's not?" Joel attacked a piece of kumara with his fork, then dropped the fork onto his plate. "I haven't done any serious practise for years, and I always get really nervous when I'm not prepared. And that time, I knew that piece inside and out, for all the good it did me."

"Pick something easier." Darin suggested. "Most of the audience won't know if you're playing something difficult."

"I'd love to hear you play." Isabel had listened to the adults quietly, frowning as she followed the conversation. "You always tell me performance isn't about how many mistakes you make but keeping going as though you hadn't made them at all."

Joel managed a smile. "I do say that, don't I?"

Marcus decided it was time to add his two cents, despite them not being worth much. "I wouldn't have a clue how difficult anything is. I'm impressed by anyone who can play."

"Thanks," Joel murmured. He flushed, picked up his fork, and pushed the defenceless piece of kumara around his plate.

"You're not the same guy you were then, and not dealing with all that crap with your dad either." Darin scowled. "I'm sure that had a lot to do with it."

Marcus frowned. Shit, whatever had happened with Joel's dad must have been major if it had affected his performance.

"Maybe." Joel bit his lip. "There's a lot riding on this concert. I can't let them down."

"If you can't do it for yourself, tell yourself you're doing it for the kids," Ella suggested.

Joe sighed. "Already tried that. It's not helping."

"So, now we've talked about the concert stuff, are you going to tell us what else is up?" Darin spoke casually, but he studied Joel with an expression of disbelief that suggested he wouldn't put up with any bullshit.

Joel glanced at Marcus and didn't say anything.

"Do you want me to leave? I'm not going to take offense if you'd prefer not to talk about something private in front of me." Marcus shrugged. "After all, you don't know me that well."

"I don't want to burden you with—" Joel started to say.

"Why don't I go find the ice cream for dessert?" Isabel said brightly. "You could help me, Uncle Marcus." She glanced at her mother. "There's ice cream, right? I saw some in the freezer last night."

Marcus hesitated. He'd meant what he said about leaving if Joel wanted to talk about something private, but he'd prefer it to be Joel's decision. Sometimes having an outside opinion about a situation could be helpful. "Joel?"

"Up to you." Joel shrugged. "Ice cream sounds wonderful, Issy. Thanks."

"I'll stay," Marcus said.

Joel waited until Isabel had left the room. "Sorry. I wasn't going to talk about it until later, but I've been on edge since Wednesday evening, and I guess it couldn't wait."

Darin nodded. Neither he nor Ella said anything, so Marcus didn't either.

"I ran into someone at the supermarket." Joel took a deep breath. "Literally ran into her with my shopping trolley. I apologised and backed off immediately of course, but…"

"But?" Ella prompted softly when Joel lapsed into silence.

"Molly Wakeman used to be my father's secretary when I was a kid." Joel took a long drink of water. "She recognised me immediately and started chatting like we'd seen each other only yesterday."

Marcus frowned. He didn't get what the issue was. "She sounds like a nice lady," he said slowly.

"Yeah, she is." Joel glanced at Marcus and then studied his plate as though Marcus had said something very wrong. "My dad and I haven't talked for years." He still didn't meet Marcus's gaze. "He threw me out of his house—and his life— when I told him I was gay."

"I'm so sorry." Marcus wasn't sure what else to say. He'd heard of others going through similar experiences, although his parents had accepted his sexuality and always been very welcoming of any partners he'd introduced. Hell, they still treated Garth like family. "That must have been... difficult," he added finally, more to break the silence than anything else.

"Claude—Joel's dad—was an arsehole about the whole thing," Darin said. "He's a very stubborn guy, much like his son."

Joel let out a breath. "Did you know my dad is having heart problems?" he asked Darin.

"Shit, no." Darin looked surprised that Joel had asked. "Why would I? I don't talk to the guy. You asked me not to, so I haven't."

"He's okay, isn't he?" Ella sounded thoughtful. "Perhaps it's time for the two of you to put the past behind you and talk about everything."

"Bernadette never said anything when we spoke on the phone a couple of days ago." Joel sounded more angry than upset. "Shit, why would my sister keep something like that from me? He's still my dad, even if he doesn't act like he is. I didn't expect to find out something like this from someone I haven't seen in years." He pushed back his chair. "Sorry. I'll be back in a few, okay?"

"Give him a few moments, and I'll go after him," Darin said. "Sorry, Marcus. Joel's the kind of guy who wears his heart on his sleeve, and despite everything, Claude is still..."

"He's still his father," Marcus finished when Darin trailed

off. "There's no need to apologise. I'd be pretty upset if I were him."

"Yeah, so would I." Darin sighed and left the table. "Finish your meal. Joel won't have gone far."

"It's fine. Take your time." He took a sip of water and then shook his head. "Poor guy," he murmured.

"Yeah." Ella poked at her vegetables but didn't eat anything. "I met Joel after he and Darin started flatting together, but anytime something happens with his family, he gets upset. It's a shame, really. Joel's a really nice guy and would do anything for anyone. He doesn't deserve to be treated like that."

"No one deserves to be treated like that." Marcus wished he could do something to help. Joel seemed like a fairly straight-up kind of guy who genuinely cared about the kids he taught. Marcus had had enough of people who said one thing and did another. Joel was a refreshing change from all that bullshit, and seeing him in pain tugged at Marcus's heartstrings.

"Yeah, I know. I've tried convincing him to talk to his dad and give it one more go, but he won't. He's never told Darin the details of what his father said, but from his reaction, it was bad. Joel and his dad used to be close, and it must be close to twenty years since they've spoken."

"Is it just his dad who has issues with him being gay?" Marcus asked.

Ella nodded. "I've met his sister a couple of times. Bernadette is nice, but she steps around the issue with their father. From what I gather, the old man has a bit of a temper on him. Joel meets up regularly with Bernadette and their mother, but that's only been in the last five years or so. He only had Darin and me as family for a very long time."

What about Reed?

Marcus almost asked the question aloud but stopped

himself in time. If Ella hadn't considered Reed as family, despite the years he'd been with Joel, there had to be a reason for it. Interesting, too, that Joel's reconciliation with his sister and mother had come around the same time he and Reed had broken up.

～

Joel glanced out the window at the morning traffic, checked his watch, and stifled a yawn. Although he hadn't been late getting home from Darin and Ella's the night before, it had taken him a while to finally drift off to sleep.

"Are you ready to order?"

The waitress, Wendy, gave him a smile that quickly turned to a frown when Joel shrugged and glanced at his watch again.

"I'm sure they'll be here soon. Why don't I get you a cup of coffee while you wait?"

"Thanks, Wendy." Joel was a regular at the Willis Street café on Saturdays, so he knew all of the waitstaff by name. "A coffee sounds good, and I'm sure they won't be long."

His phone alerted him to a new text from his sister.

Nearly there. Delayed by accident near the Newlands turnoff. Looking for a car park now.

He sent a smiley face as a reply and closed his phone. Wendy set a cup of coffee in front of him, and he sipped it slowly.

His sister and mother both lived in Tawa, so usually they took it in turns to drive to the twice-monthly Saturday brunches. They'd settled on Wellington city as their meeting place since it was a midpoint for both of them. Joel had offered to meet them somewhere in Tawa, but his mother, Jill, had insisted this would be more convenient.

Joel suspected it had less to do with convenience and

more to do with the fact his father didn't come into the city on Saturdays, as he preferred to spend it watching one of the local rugby games. The time and location gave his mother the chance to see Joel without having to tell his father about it.

His mother had always been a bit on the passive-aggressive side. Meeting a problem head-on had never been her style. After Joel left home, it had taken her years to contact him directly, and even then, she'd never talked about why he'd moved out. Joel suspected his sister had set up that first meeting, but she'd never admitted to it, and Joel hadn't asked.

Although he usually preferred to know where he stood, this was one of the few circumstances in which ignorance was bliss.

Jill had stayed clear of the argument between her husband and son too. Joel often wondered why she'd never stood up for him, but then she hadn't taken her husband's side either or voiced her opinion of the situation.

Joel had never discussed his sexuality with his mother. Every time he'd mentioned Reed, she'd changed the subject or referred to him as Joel's friend. They'd never met. Reed hadn't bothered to make the effort, despite Joel's nervousness about making contact with his mother again. In hindsight it was another clue that his and Reed's relationship wasn't working as well as Joel wanted to believe it was. Two brunches in, and Joel was single again, giving him one less awkward conversation to worry about.

"Joel!" Bernadette called his name from the doorway and then stopped to exchange a few words with Wendy before sitting down opposite Joel. He'd chosen a table inside the café, rather than out on the pavement as he did usually. The café was quiet at present, but it got busy closer to lunchtime. A music shop had originally stood at the location, and the themed mural on one wall of the café depicted musical notation and various instruments against a backdrop of the harbour.

Joel found it relaxing, and he suspected Bernadette had chosen the location because of their shared love of music. She had played viola years ago, but while Joel pursued music as a career, Bernadette studied business. She still owned her instrument but hadn't touched it since she'd left home for university.

"Where's Mum?" Joel asked.

"Her phone rang when I was feeding the meter, so she told me to go on ahead." Bernadette studied the menu, although she ordered the same thing every time.

"Good. It gives us time to talk first before she gets here."

Bernadette peered over the menu and raised an eyebrow. "What's up? You look tired. Not sleeping well?"

"No idea why that would be. Do you?" Joel tilted his head to the side and glared at her. So much for his intention to slide the topic of his father into the conversation subtly, and after they'd been talking a while.

"Why would I?" Bernadette studied him for a moment and then brushed a lock of blonde hair from her face. While Joel took after his father with his dark hair, Bernadette was blonde like their mother, although both siblings had inherited their father's bright blue eyes.

"I ran into Mrs Wakeman at the supermarket a couple of days ago, and she told me about Dad." Joel gave Wendy a nod as she set down a cup of chai latte in front of Bernadette. "Thanks, Wendy," he said before Bernadette could say anything.

"Yes, thanks, Wendy," Bernadette echoed. "He's fine, Joel, honest," she said once Wendy had left their table. "If it was something serious, I would have phoned you immediately."

"Would you?" Joel asked more coldly than he'd intended.

"Of course I would." Bernadette briefly put her hand over

Joel's, then removed it when he didn't acknowledge the gesture.

Joel knew he was acting like an arsehole, but, hell, this hurt. "Mrs Wakeman presumed I already knew. How many other people knew before I did? He's still my father, Bernie."

"Would you have dropped everything and rushed to his bedside if I'd rung you?" Bernadette matched Joel's cool tone. She snorted when he shrugged. "I didn't think so. Honestly, the two of you are so alike. One of you needs to back down on this thing." She turned towards the door when the jangle of a bell signalled the arrival of their mother. "I'm tired of this whole elephant in the room. It's gone on long enough."

"He could apologise." Joel scowled. "I didn't walk out. He threw me out, and how the hell do *I* back down? I'm gay. It's not as though I'm going to stop being gay because he doesn't like it."

"Yes, I know that, but—"

"Do you? You were away at uni in Otago when it happened. You didn't hear what he said." Joel shrugged and crossed his arms over his chest.

Bernadette had met her husband while they'd both been at uni and settled in Christchurch with him after they'd got married. She'd moved back to Wellington ten years ago and hadn't made much of an effort to meet up in person with Joel until six months before Reed had left for Australia. Reed and Bernadette hadn't got along, so Joel found it easier to avoid situations that meant they'd have to all be together. He and his sister had spent too many years conversing via texting and emailing while trying to avoid the two elephants in the room—Joel's partner and their father's disapproval of Joel's sexuality.

"Morning, Mum." Joel looked up as his mother approached their table. "Do you want me to order you some tea?"

Jill sat down next to Bernadette and glanced between her children. "Oh dear. You've been arguing, haven't you? I do wish you wouldn't do that."

"We're not five years old anymore," Bernadette mumbled. "I'll order you a pot of tea, and Joel can fill you in." She gave Joel a not-quite-apologetic smile and then bolted towards the counter instead of waving the waitress over.

"Coward," Joel muttered. "How's Dad?" he asked his mother.

"He's fine." Jill gave her quick casual answer then shrugged off her coat and hung it on the back of her chair. After she sat down, she looked up and met Joel's gaze. "Oh," she said. "You heard about his heart? It was a warning he needs to slow down, that's all. You know how hard your father works, and he's been very busy lately, especially after that last earthquake."

Claude Ashcroft owned a construction company. As well as building new homes and business premises, the company also had a reputation for good quality refurbishment of older buildings, especially those classified as heritage. After the Christchurch earthquakes, they'd had plenty of work as companies scrambled to get their buildings up to spec. The more recent Kaikoura earthquake had revealed even more buildings in Wellington that needed strengthening. Claude tended to oversee most of his company's work. He'd never been good at delegating.

"Is he going to slow down?" Joel asked.

"It's Dad." Bernadette slid back into her seat. "Of course he's not. I've ordered you some tea," she told her mother.

"Thank you." Jill picked up the menu and peered at it. "I'll have an omelette today," she said as though she was ordering something new rather than the same thing she had every time they ate there.

Wendy walked over to them with her notepad. "I see

you're ready to order. So that's the same as usual for you, Mrs Ashcroft?" She wrote down the order. "And for you, Bernadette?"

Bernadette nodded. "Yes, thank you."

"I'll have the big breakfast," Joel said.

"You're skipping lunch again, aren't you?" Jill asked, peering at him over the top of her glasses.

"This is meant to be brunch," he pointed out. "But yes, I have a lot of work to do today. We're having a fundraising concert at school in a few months. I need to organise the music for the choir and the orchestra so we can start rehearsals."

"Don't work too hard." Jill sighed. "I do worry about you, Joel. You've done nothing but work since your friend Reed left." She shook her head. "From the way you talked about him, I thought the two of you were such good friends. It's a shame he got that job offer in Australia."

"He wasn't just my friend, Mum. He was my boyfriend." Joel couldn't be bothered sidestepping that fact any longer. After the week he'd had, he wasn't in the mood.

To his surprise, Jill rolled her eyes. "I know that, dear. You seemed happy when you were together. I'm hoping you won't be alone for too long—especially as it's been five years already. It's not good to be alone, you know." She smiled at Bernadette. "I see your sister happy and settled with her Keith and their boys. Of course I want the same thing for you."

"You've never given me that impression before," Joel mumbled.

"Oh, and you must let me know when your concert is," Jill continued as though he hadn't said anything. "It's been so long since I've been to a concert, and—"

"I appreciate you wanting to come, but it's really not necessary." The last thing Joel wanted was his mother in the audience. Especially as he had to psych himself up to play solo.

Jill beamed. "Of course it is!" She leaned in closer as though she was about to reveal some deep and dark secret. "I know your father is going to be fine, but I'm seeing this as a warning to both of us. After all, none of us know how long we have, and I've missed so many years of your life. It's time I made up for that, don't you think?"

CHAPTER FOUR

Marcus stopped the lawn mower engine and took off his earmuffs. He stretched his shoulders and wandered over to his water bottle. The sun had come out midmorning, and the day was warming up to be much hotter than he'd expected.

He'd felt awkward intruding on something private the night before, despite Joel telling him he could stay. When Joel finally returned to the dinner table Darin—not very subtly—had changed the subject. Still, Joel remained quiet for most of the evening. Marcus hated seeing Joel so upset, yet not knowing Joel well, he'd been wary about making the situation worse. He'd found it easier not to say anything at all, especially as he'd never been one for small talk.

Ella had told him that Joel would be meeting his mother and sister for brunch late the next morning, so Marcus figured it would be a good time to mow his lawns. At least if the brunch didn't go well, Joel would come home to one less job to do.

He retrieved his bottle from the wooden table, took a long drink, and then sat in a nearby chair. Marcus smiled as he surveyed his work. Joel's neatly mowed back lawn looked much better now. He had a decent-sized section—not too large yet big enough to lounge outside on a warm summer evening. Marcus could imagine Joel out here, listening to music while he worked on his laptop, or perhaps took some time out to read a book.

What kind of books did Joel like to read? Would he be interested in the book Marcus had nearly finished? One of the things Marcus loved about reading was discussing the books afterwards. Garth enjoyed reading too, although they had very different taste in fiction. Marcus enjoyed a good thriller, while Garth preferred fantasy. They'd often sat curled on the sofa together after a long day, reading paragraphs or sentences to each other that had caught their eye.

He missed that. It was the little things he hadn't thought about before their breakup that hit him the hardest and reminded him he wasn't part of a couple anymore.

"Hello there!" A woman called a greeting over the side fence.

Marcus got up and walked over to her. "Hello there." The fence was about his height. He tested the strength of the old rotting bench seat in front of it and then climbed onto it so he could introduce himself properly. "I'm Marcus. I'm mowing Mr Ashcroft's lawns while he's out."

"Nice to meet you." The woman appeared to be in her late seventies and wore a large-brimmed straw hat. "I'm Mrs Morris—Mavis. We like to know what's going on in this neighbourhood and look out for one another, you know. There are so many people out there getting into trouble as they have too much time on their hands, so it pays to be careful. Joel's a good boy; he's been very kind to me since he moved in." She looked Marcus up and down. "You were here last week with his niece... Isabel, isn't it?"

"Yes, that's right." Marcus didn't see the harm in confirming what she already knew. Isabel wasn't exactly

Joel's niece, but he wasn't going to correct her assumption. "Isabel's mother is my sister, so you'll probably see me around here a bit more too."

He and Joel had sort of agreed that it was okay for Marcus to take on the lawn mowing, although they hadn't formally discussed any details.

"Of course." Mavis smiled. "I didn't know Joel had arranged for someone to mow his lawns, but I've been telling him he needs to get someone in. He doesn't really have the time himself, and he does look so tired sometimes." She lowered her voice. "It's good to know there's someone looking out for him."

"I mow lawns for a living." Marcus didn't want her to get the wrong idea. Although it was an idea he had to admit he rather liked. He'd enjoy getting to know Joel better. Just as friends, of course.

Because he wouldn't presume anything else.

"Uh-huh." Mavis nodded. "I'd better let you get back to work, then. Still, it's nice to meet you. I thought the other day that you seemed like a very pleasant young man."

"Thanks." Marcus cleared his throat. "I'd better get back to work." He echoed her earlier words. "I still have the edges to do before Joel gets home." He turned to go.

"Oh… Marcus." Mavis called him back.

"Yes, Mrs Morris?"

"Call me Mavis. You said you mowed lawns for a living? I don't suppose you could fit another client in, and if so, do you have a card or something?"

"I don't have any business cards on me. Tell you what. I can pop over later in the week and give you a quote. If you're out, I'll leave the quote and my card in your letter box. How does that sound?"

"Perfect. I'll look forward to hearing from you. Thanks, dear."

"Thanks, Mavis." Marcus watched her walk back over to her clothesline. She'd been outside hanging washing and must have heard the lawn mower, or more likely she'd seen him arrive earlier when she'd been peering through the curtains in her front room. It appeared that Neighbourhood Watch was alive and well in Waterloo.

One more swig from his water bottle emptied it completely. Marcus glanced at his watch. Still plenty of time to get everything done and be gone by the time Joel got home.

~

Joel pulled into his driveway and got out of the car. He opened the boot, retrieved the crate filled with the student work he needed to mark, and frowned.

Something looked different.

The edge of the curtain from next door fell in a hurry. Mavis always had to know what was going on. Some of his neighbours thought she was nosy, but Joel liked her. She reminded him of his grandmother, who had died years ago. Nana Ashcroft had always made it her business to know what was going on, yet if anything happened, she'd be there in the thick of it, helping out.

Hang on. Who owned the SUV parked outside? He read the side of it. Brendan Jarratt. Lawns and section clearing. No job too big or too small.

The penny dropped. His lawns had been mowed. But he hadn't made any specific arrangements for that to happen. Sure, he and Marcus had talked about it, although they hadn't gone further than that.

Joel opened his front door and dumped the crate on the table. He glanced out the window and froze.

Marcus was mopping his face with his shirt, the muscles

in his bare back flexing as he moved. Joel swallowed, his mouth suddenly dry.

Oh God. He licked his lips. He'd thought Marcus was ripped, but actually seeing it in the… flesh…

Joel grew hard.

Marcus turned. A slow blush spread across his equally bare chest when he saw Joel. He pulled his T-shirt back over his head.

Shit. Don't do that!

Nannerl rubbed herself around Joel's legs and meowed loudly. "Don't worry, kitty," he said absently. "I'm not going to let him get away."

Joel froze, mortified. What the hell had possessed him to say that? He barely knew Marcus, and definitely not well enough to… Shit, Marcus hit all of Joel's buttons with that physique. He'd always liked his men with a few muscles, although not overly so. Add to that the lovely, tanned skin— how far down did that tan go?

The loud rap on the back door made him jump. He sprinted to the door and opened it.

"Sorry. I kind of hoped to have finished before you got home." Marcus indicated the freshly mowed back lawn. "I know we didn't discuss any details the other day, but I figured as I had a free morning I'd get started. I hope you don't mind."

"Oh, right." Joel pulled himself up sharply. "Of course I don't mind." He wished he'd got home earlier and been able to watch Marcus work. He forced himself to stop staring at Marcus's abs and shifted his focus to the empty water bottle in his hand. "Umm, thanks. Would you like me to refill your bottle? It's… hot as today." He fell back on the Kiwi tendency to use *as* when his brain refused to supply a suitable comparative word.

"Yeah, thanks. I can wait outside." Marcus indicated his

boots. "I'm sure you don't want me to traipse grass inside."

"It's fine." Joel turned towards the kitchen. "It's just floor-boards in this part of the house, and I haven't washed the floors this weekend yet."

He heard footsteps behind him as Marcus followed him through the laundry into the kitchen.

"Tap water or cold out of the fridge?"

"Out of the fridge, thanks."

"There you go." Joel handed the refilled water bottle to Marcus. Their fingers brushed, Marcus's skin, warm against Joel's. "Leave me the bill, and I'll get it paid ASAP. Do you prefer cash or internet banking?"

"The first time is on the house." Marcus finished his water and turned the neck of the bottle this way and that. He looked as though he wanted to say something but couldn't decide whether he should or not.

"I won't bite. If there's something else you want to say, I figure it's better to say it, right?" God, had Marcus seen him ogling his muscles through the window? Surely he wouldn't have an issue with it. After all, it wasn't as though Joel had actually done anything. And Marcus was definitely gay. He'd had a boyfriend.

Had. As in past tense.

Joel poured himself a glass of water and drank it slowly to give Marcus time to gather his thoughts. He wasn't a guy who ran off at the mouth like Joel did, that was for sure.

"I was worried about you last night," Marcus said finally. "You seemed really upset, and I wanted to help." He squeezed the bottle with one hand, leaving a dent in the plastic. Joel watched the bottle slowly expand into its proper shape. "I think it sucks that your dad has issues with you being gay. No one should go through that shit."

"Thanks." Joel figured he should say something a little more intelligent, although he got the impression Marcus didn't expect him to. "Your parents didn't have an issue with it? You being gay, I mean."

"No." Marcus smiled as though remembering. "The opposite really. They were very supportive and had already guessed, although they waited for me to get up the courage to tell them."

"That's nice." Joel let out a long breath. "Sorry, I don't mean to sound trite, but…"

"It's okay." Marcus tilted his head to the side and studied Joel for a moment. "As I said, I was concerned, and if you ever need someone to talk to and all that… I'm not much of a conversationalist, but I've been told I listen well."

"I think you're a great conversationalist."

Thankfully at that point, Nannerl sat down in front of the fridge and provided a well-timed distraction.

"I think your cat wants to be fed."

"She always wants to be fed." Joel realised he was still holding his glass. He put it down on the counter next to the fridge. "Thanks again for mowing the lawns."

"No problem."

Marcus bent to pet Nannerl, who purred loudly. He smiled, his eyes crinkling up at the edges. The colour reminded Joel of clouds on a stormy day just before it rained.

"I'd better be going," Marcus said. "You've probably got a lot of work to catch up on, especially with this concert to prepare for."

"Concert? Oh, yes. I guess I do." Joel returned Marcus's smile. "Thanks again for doing the lawns. They look great. Do you need a hand packing up?"

"No, it's fine. All part of the service." Marcus headed for the door, then turned when he reached the doorframe. "Would you like me to keep doing them? It's fine if you'd prefer I didn't. As I said, I was just helping out today."

"Yes. Thanks. I mean yes, please. I'd love it if you keep

doing them. I don't have much time, and at least this way it's only the garden that looks wild." Joel remembered Marcus saying he gardened as well, but Joel wasn't about to ask him to take on that too.

"Okay. That's settled, then. See you later."

"See you later." Joel waited until Marcus left and then shut the door behind him.

God, awkward much? Joel had gone between not saying much at all to babbling like an idiot, like he'd done the first time they'd met. No wonder Marcus had timed his mowing when Joel was out.

Marcus busied himself packing up. He didn't dare look back at the house. What must Joel think of his offer to listen to him talk about something very personal?

Mavis had quickly moved away from her window as soon as he'd left the house. Probably wondering why he'd gone inside. Well, she could keep wondering.

Joel had watched him earlier too, but Marcus wasn't sure what to make of that. Joel had seemed embarrassed when he'd seen Marcus without his shirt, but that didn't mean anything. It wasn't *going* to mean anything.

That smile Joel had given him in the kitchen made Marcus feel warm inside. Garth's smiles had always given the impression he was party to some joke Marcus didn't know about. Joel's had felt genuine, and his eyes twinkled as his lips curled up into an almost grin. It was obvious as hell Nannerl adored him, and cats were usually a good judge of character. Not only that, but the cat had taken a liking to Marcus too.

He missed having a cat. Garth had kept theirs—it made more sense as they'd been living on the farm, and it was her home.

He sighed and hefted the mower onto the back of the SUV.

But Marcus wasn't ready for another relationship just yet… He had to find his feet in a new town, and with Joel being a close family friend, if things didn't work out, the situation would get very awkward very quickly.

Maybe what Joel needed right now was a friend. If that was the case, Marcus could be that for him, no problem. He smiled at the thought of getting to know Joel better. His mother had always said that making friends was important, and it never hurt to make new ones. Marcus hadn't done much of that for a while. His life for a very long time had revolved around his work—and Garth.

The ignition on the SUV coughed and spluttered sluggishly, struggling to turn over, but within moments was running fine. Brendan had recently bought a new vehicle, and Marcus had brought his old one at a decent price. It had behaved fine up to now, so hopefully it was a one-off glitch. He'd get Darin to take a look at the SUV if it played up again. Brendan also had a spare mower and weed eater as his son had helped out on occasion when things had been busy in the past, so borrowing them until they figured out how to split the workload wasn't an issue.

Marcus gave Joel's house another glance before heading home to get on with the rest of his weekend. Starting on Ella's garden would take care of the rest of the day. He'd promised Isabel he'd take her into Oriental Bay on Sunday and they could walk along the beach after buying ice creams. She was looking forward to the train ride and had hinted about looking at some new exhibition at Te Papa.

He was already part of a family here and wasn't lonely. He didn't need another relationship.

But that didn't mean he and Joel couldn't become friends.

~

Joel had started work as soon as Marcus had left the day before, taken a short break to eat dinner, then finally had to call it a night when he couldn't make sense of the words on the screen. His progress hadn't improved much since he'd started back into it early this morning and he was already getting tired of the sight of his laptop.

It took a while for him to register that the music he could hear wasn't coming from his stereo. He picked up his phone and smiled at the familiar name on the screen. "Hi, Issy. What's up?"

"Hi, Uncle Joel." Isabel sounded very cheerful, perhaps a little too much so. "Dad said I could phone you after two because you'd need a break by then so you don't work too hard. It's one minute past two now. That's okay, isn't it?"

"Of course it is." Joel waited for the other shoe to drop. "Is everything all right?"

Isabel lowered her voice to a dramatic whisper. "I'm in town, and we're having ice creams. Do you want to come have ice cream with us?"

Joel glanced at the pile of paperwork he had to finish. It could wait until that evening, and he would probably get through it faster if he took a break now.

"Are you sure you don't mind me intruding?" Joel didn't want to butt into quality father/daughter time. He knew how busy Darin was with work.

"Of course not!" Isabel sounded positively gleeful. "We're leaving Te Papa now, and we're heading around to Oriental Bay. We could meet you by Freyberg Pool and walk the rest of the way to Kaffee Eis together. They have really yummy gelato ice creams."

"Okay, see you soon." Joel saved the file he was working on and closed his laptop. He grabbed his wallet and headed out the door. Nannerl glanced at him from her favourite spot under one of the bushes by the front door, then went back to sleep again.

He reached for a CD to listen to, then decided on the radio instead. Hearing the voices of the DJs gave the illusion of having company for the drive, and he was in the mood for some humorous banter. He'd chosen some music for the concert, but the only arrangements available for orchestra were too difficult for the kids to play. He'd have to simplify them, but not too much. His students would enjoy a challenge, but if the music was *too* difficult, it would scare them off.

The traffic wasn't bad for a Sunday afternoon, and he was soon on the motorway heading to Wellington. People sunbathed on the beach, and kids splashed in the water with their parents. One of these days, he'd find the time to go swimming in the sea again. He hadn't done it in years, but the warm weather made the glistening water seem very inviting.

A train rambled past him as he changed lanes. Another ten minutes and a couple of red traffic lights later, Joel approached Oriental Bay. Finding a car park took a bit longer than he'd expected, so he had a good five-minute walk to reach the pool. He dug out his phone and sent Isabel a quick text with his ETA.

Joel let out a contented sigh as he walked. This was exactly what he'd needed. A few minutes out in the sunlight and the feel of the cool sea breeze against his skin washed away all the tension of the afternoon. By the time he was a couple of hundred metres from the pool, he'd decided he needed to schedule some downtime into his weekend, even if it was only a walk along the beach and sitting on the wall watching children playing in the sand. He'd buried himself in his work for too long and forgotten what it meant to stop and smell the flowers, or in this case, the brisk scent of the ocean on a summer's day.

He saw Isabel waving and sped up his pace. "Issy!" he called.

The man standing with her, looking out at the ocean, turned in surprise as Joel approached. "Joel. What a pleasant surprise. What are you doing here?"

Joel skidded to a halt. "Marcus? I didn't know you were here with Darin and Isabel." It was a nice surprise but odd that Isabel hadn't mentioned it.

"Darin?" Marcus frowned. "Darin's at home with Ella. It's just me and Isabel here." He gave his niece a look. "This isn't a coincidence, is it?"

"Why, Uncle Marcus, I don't know what you mean. I never told Uncle Joel I was out with Dad. If he made that assumption, it's hardly my fault."

"Of course it's not." Joel smelt a child-sized rat. "Sorry, Marcus. She invited me here, but I thought it was to have ice cream with her and Darin."

Marcus gave Joel a repeat of the smile from the day before, and his voice suddenly softened. "Is it a problem that it's with me instead?"

Joel ignored the way his heart sped up in response. "No," he said, his mouth suddenly too dry. "No, of course not. It's perfect weather for an ice cream and a walk on the beach, and this break from work is exactly what I need."

"It's beautiful here." Marcus rolled his eyes as Isabel ran a short distance ahead to less-than-subtly give them some time alone. "Busy, but peaceful at the same time. Do you come here often?"

"I used to, but it's been a while." Joel figured he'd better start walking to catch up with Isabel at the crossing. "Life's been busy, and it's not always easy to take some time out."

"I know that feeling." Marcus brushed his shoulder

against Joel's and then awkwardly put more distance between them. "I've spent a lot of time working lately, and I keep forgetting to appreciate the world around me." The wind tugged at his hair, and he brushed it back from his face in a subconscious, yet graceful gesture that made him look almost vulnerable.

"I've been told it's important to make time." Joel shrugged. "Easier said than done, though."

"Yeah, I've heard that one too." Marcus chuckled, and his eyes twinkled. He seemed more relaxed than Joel had seen him before. "It wouldn't have been my sister who imparted those words of wisdom, would it?"

"How did you guess?" Joel edged closer again, enjoying the easy conversation.

On the beach to their left, a child giggled. Joel glanced over as the girl placed a pretty shell on the top of a huge sandcastle. She looked up at him and then said something to the older boy with her.

Joel recognised them from school and picked up his pace. He didn't want work intruding into what was shaping up to be a perfect afternoon.

If Marcus noticed Joel's reaction, he didn't show it. "I've been told there are loads of ice cream flavours to choose from," he said as they caught up with Isabel. "What do you recommend?"

"Huh?" Joel checked the road for traffic before they crossed.

"What's your favourite flavour ice cream?" Isabel said.

"They might have new ones." Joel sidestepped the question as his mind helpfully provided an image of Marcus licking an ice cream, his tongue curling around the cold gelato. "Oh look, we're here already." He led the way into the shop and deliberately shoved the lovely Technicolour visual from his mind.

The girl behind the counter smiled when they came in. "Good afternoon. What can I help you with today?"

"I'll have a strawberry cone, please." Isabel ordered first. "Uncle Marcus?"

Joel felt Marcus's gaze on his back and moved over to let him peruse the flavours. There must have been at least two dozen to choose from, maybe more.

"I'm still thinking." Marcus took a step closer. He licked his lips, then swallowed hard.

The action went straight to Joel's groin. He cleared his throat. "Biscotti, please. I haven't had it before, and it looks good."

"It's one of my favourites. Good choice." The girl handed Isabel her cone and then began to fix Joel's.

"I'd like what you have—you're having." Marcus leaned in closer, peered into the cabinet, and then gave Joel a warm smile. "I agree. It does look good."

So do you. Joel couldn't help returning the smile. Marcus had a wonderful natural scent, with an underlying smell of apple, probably from whatever shampoo he'd used that morning.

"Do you want to find a seat, or walk along the beach?" Marcus asked after they left the shop.

"Either works." Joel glanced at Isabel who shrugged. His decision, then. Okay. "Walking along the beach sounds good. It's warm enough to go for a paddle if you'd like."

"How long since you've been here?" Marcus licked the top of his gelato, his tongue curling as he systematically attacked it. A tiny bit trickled down the cone onto his fingers, and he sucked them clean.

Joel swallowed, and took a bite off his, the sudden cold settling in his chest. He coughed, Marcus watching him closely.

"You okay?"

"Yeah, fine." Joel glanced at Isabel who was skipping ahead of them, then back at Marcus. "It's been a while since I took a break," he admitted. "I was thinking on the walk here that I should do it more often."

"Walking by the shore is good for the soul." Marcus dropped one hand, his fingers brushing against Joel. He didn't acknowledge what he'd done so, not wanting to spoil the mood, Joel didn't tell him.

"I used to walk along the beach at Petone a lot when I needed space to think." Joel looked up the gulls circling overhead. "The waves have their own music, if you listen hard enough."

"I hadn't thought of it that way." Marcus stilled and studied the sea, its steady rhythm caressing the shore, then retreating. "I like the reliability of the tides. I used to fish on the river before I…" He faltered.

"Did you catch much?" Joel smoothed over the break in Marcus's story, recognising the sad, yet resigned look in his eyes. He'd felt that way for months after Reed, and it hadn't been as long since Marcus's breakup.

"A bit of trout, and very occasionally I saw some salmon." Marcus raised his voice. "Issy, don't get too far ahead!"

Isabel had run to catch up with a group of children her own age. How many kids from the school were out here today?

"Perhaps we could sit and watch her spend some time with her friends?" Joel gestured to an empty bench seat facing the beach.

Patricia—one of the mothers with the group of children approached them before Marcus had the chance to reply. "Hi, Mr Ashcroft. We're staying here a while longer, and Isabel is welcome to join us if you'd like." Her husband waved to Joel from a couple of benches over, and he waved back. "Good for the kids to get some sun before the weather deteriorates again."

"She's here with her uncle, Mr Verden, actually. But if they're both okay with the idea, that would be fine. Thanks."

Isabel waved to them, a pleading look on her face.

"Nice to meet you, Mr Verden." Patricia held out her hand and Marcus shook it. "Mr Ashcroft will vouch for us. Our eldest two are in his classes, with the other set to invade in a year or two."

Marcus chuckled. "It's Marcus, and I'm not going to stand in the way of my niece having fun with her friends, if you're sure it's no trouble."

"No trouble at all. Do you want to trade numbers and meet back here in an hour?" Patricia suggested. "The kids want to play on the beach for a while."

"Sounds good." Marcus swapped contact details with her. "Thanks. Text me if you change your mind and want to get going sooner."

"Sure. Enjoy your peace and quiet." Patricia sprinted back to the group of half a dozen children. Each of her four children had a friend with them, so Isabel made nine.

"Do you want to stay here, or walk on the beach?" Joel asked.

"Walk on the beach I'm thinking." Marcus decided. "If that's still okay with you," he added.

"Very okay." Joel finished off the last of his ice cream, then munched on the cone. Marcus swallowed, then mirrored Joel's action.

"Your ex was an idiot," he murmured.

Joel raised an eyebrow. "You've been talking to Darin, I see."

"Just an observation." Marcus shrugged. "Any spots on the beach I should see, or any preference for direction?"

"Not really." Joel fought the urge to slip his hand into

Marcus's as they walked along side by side. "You and your ex liked to fish? Sometimes it's difficult to get back into something you used to do together."

"He hated it." Marcus smoothed the sand in front of him with one shoe. "Then life got busy and I gave it up. It's not something you can do in five minutes, so it was easier to spend the time doing something we both enjoyed."

"Maybe it's something you could take up again?"

"Maybe." Marcus found a stone amongst the shells and walked down to the shoreline. He skimmed it across the waves. It jumped a couple of times and then sunk to the bottom. "I have a business to grow, and that's going to take a bit of time."

"Yeah, it will." Joel shaded his eyes as he looked out across the harbour.

The sun caught Marcus's hair in a warm glow. His thigh muscles flexed as he crouched by the edge of the water.

Joel hesitated, knelt next to Marcus. and placed his hand on Marcus's shoulder. Marcus turned to face him and frowned.

"I'm not—"

Joel chose his words carefully, ignoring his racing heart. "It's hard starting over again. I just… I thought perhaps you could use a friend."

Marcus froze then nodded slowly. "I could do that, and I'd like that. I'd like that a lot." His voice faltered. "Thank you."

CHAPTER FIVE

"Sorry, I'm late." Marcus took his seat at the dinner table. "I raced to get that last job finished before the rain hit. Don't worry, I've cleaned up, but I haven't had time to change." Luckily, he was wearing shorts, so he didn't have wet jeans to deal with, and his jacket had protected him from getting soaked.

"You're fine the way you are, and we're not eating until Joel arrives, so dinner is keeping warm in the oven until then." Ella glanced at her watch and frowned. "Darin, have you heard from Joel? He's usually here by now."

"Hang on, I thought I heard my phone when I was dropping Isabel off at Sophie's." Darin walked over to the kitchen bench and checked his phone. "Rehearsal ran late. He's coming straight from school and on his way. Sorry, should have looked earlier."

"It's hosing down out there." Marcus winced when a roll of thunder shook the house. Joel would have to park on the road as Marcus had left his SUV in the driveway behind Darin's car. "Perhaps I could meet him with an umbrella."

Ella and Darin glanced at each other. Ella grinned. "With

the way the wind is today? You'd end up doing a Mary Poppins impression, and as amusing as that would be, it's not a great idea."

"A little bit of rain isn't going to hurt him," Darin added. "It's sweet the way you're worried about him, though."

"He needs someone to worry about him," Marcus said without thinking.

Darin raised an eyebrow.

"Apart from you guys, I meant. Of course."

"Of course." Ella's grin widened. "I'm very happy that you two are getting along so well."

"We're friends."

Marcus had meant to ask Joel out for coffee—as a friend asking another friend to meet up—but hadn't had the time since they'd met up for ice cream a few weeks ago. The only weekend he'd been free, Joel hadn't so they'd settled for chatting briefly after Isabel's lessons, at weekly Friday night dinners, and sending a few texts in between.

"Friends look out for each other," he added, giving Ella a pointed look.

Ella laughed. "Yes, yes they do."

"That sounds like him now." Darin peered outside. "Marcus, do you want to open the door for Joel while I go find him some dry clothes."

"Sure." Marcus sprinted for the front door, not wanting Joel to be out in the rain any longer than he had to.

By the time Joel reached the house he was soaked through. He dived through the door, dripping puddles onto the mat. He shook out the sweatshirt he'd held over his head as a makeshift barrier against the rain. "Forgot my jacket this morning."

"You're sopping. Darin's gone to get you some dry clothes."

Joel's t-shirt clung to him, accentuating his chest and

firm, round nipples. The thin material didn't leave much to the imagination. Marcus stared at him... and swallowed. Joel's hair hung over his face in wet clumps. Marcus brushed it off Joel's face without thinking.

Joel stilled, his lips parted. Time slowed, then Joel took a step back. "I'm dripping all over the floor. Ella will have a fit."

The moment broken, Marcus managed a nod. "Yes... I mean, no. I'm sure she won't. I'll get you a towel." He bolted down the hallway to the linen cupboard, nearly walking into Darin. "Joel. Towel."

"Right." Darin sounded amused. "Told you he'd be wet." He handed Marcus a towel. "Give him that—and tell him he's welcome to a hot shower if he'd like one. I'll be there in a moment with some dry clothes for him."

"Okay." Marcus bit his lip, pushing away the visual of Joel in the shower, or naked in the bathroom drying himself off. "I'll do that. Um, tell him, I mean."

Darin grinned. "I think we both know what you meant."

Replying would only open himself to more teasing so Marcus collected what was left of his dignity and took the towel back to Joel. "Help yourself to a shower. Darin's bringing clothes. I'll make you some tea to help warm you through." He hesitated. "Unless you'd prefer coffee?"

"Tea is fine, thanks." Joel started to dry his hair. "See you in a bit. Thanks." He headed for the bathroom.

Ella was waiting for Marcus in the kitchen. "Joel's a good-looking guy."

"I never said he wasn't." Marcus filled up the kettle and spooned some tea into the pot. He glanced around to make sure Darin wasn't in earshot and lowered his voice. "I'm not ready for another relationship. I've already told you that."

"Yeah, you have." Ella got the milk out of the fridge. "Keep your options open, though. I think you and Joel would be good together, so don't dismiss the possibility offhand. If it's meant to be it will happen."

"I guess." Each time he saw Joel, it grew more difficult for Marcus to ignore his attraction to him.

"Be yourself and let things happen, hmm?" Ella grimaced. "And don't let what happened with Garth put you off trying again. I never did see what you saw in him."

"Yeah, you've told me that." Marcus had lost count of the number of times she had.

She studied him. "You're looking much more rested, and you've put weight on again since you got here. I'd like to think it's living with us and my good cooking, but I think it's more than that."

"What's more than that?" Joel walked into the kitchen.

"Ella was reminding me how good her cooking is." Marcus glanced at Joel. Shit, the t-shirt he wore was at least one size too small, and fitted very snugly. Marcus was thankful his shorts were baggy and hid his reaction. First the wet t-shirt, and now this.

Let things happen my arse. Darin was a similar build to Joel, but this shirt was one of Ella's. Darin and Ella needed a few pointers on subtlety. They meant well but...

"Why don't you both head into the living room?" Ella said brightly, "I'll get Darin to call you when dinner is served."

"I can help—" Marcus started to say.

She handed Joel two mugs of tea. "Go drink your tea, and warm up. Do you want me to find you a dry sweatshirt too?"

"No, I'm fine." Joel looked Marcus up and down. His grip tightened on the mugs. "It's not that cold, now that I'm dry."

Marcus shrugged, and went to follow Joel into the living room, only to find he'd paused in the doorway, leaning against the door to keep it open. He gave Marcus one of the cups.

"You didn't have to get changed for dinner."

"I didn't." Marcus frowned, unsure what Joel's point was. "It's warmer today and I was in a hurry, so I didn't have time to change."

"Oh." Joel hesitated, then smiled. "Well, you should wear shorts more often, then."

"I guess." Was Joel flirting with him?

"Your t-shirt is very…"

Joel flushed. "That's Darin's fault, not mine." He headed for the open fire, goose bumps covering his arms. Marcus handed him one of the throws Ella kept over the loveseat. "Thanks." Joel placed his cup on the mantelpiece while he draped the blanket over his shoulders, then sipped his tea. "I feel like an idiot forgetting my jacket this morning. I know how quickly the weather can change."

"You're far from an idiot," Marcus said softly, disappointed by the change of subject. Joel had offered friendship, nothing more. Noticing how hot he was didn't mean they had to fall into bed together, or ruin what they were slowly building between them by doing so.

Shit. It had been far too long since Marcus had been laid.

"Definitely distracted, then." Joel stared into the flames. "I knew going into it that this concert would be a lot of work, but I swear some of these kids aren't practising at all between rehearsals."

"They're kids. It kind of goes with the territory." Marcus sat on the loveseat so he wouldn't be tempted to place a comforting arm around Joel. "I seem to remember a text from you only a few days ago, telling me the other day that it would all come together the week before the concert."

"Yeah, I did say that, didn't I?" Joel perched on the arm of the seat next to Marcus. "At least it's the weekend. Gives me time to do some practising myself."

Marcus raised an eyebrow. "You're taking some time out,

though?" Perhaps he should kidnap Joel and drag him out for that coffee.

"Maybe." Joel looked sheepish. "I don't have a lot of time and..."

"I'll pick you up at three tomorrow," Marcus said firmly.

"Excuse me?"

"That will give you the morning and a good part of the afternoon to work, and then I'll take you out for afternoon tea. You'll need a break by then."

"Are you asking me out?" Joel raised an eyebrow. "I thought we—"

"We are. Friends make sure friends take breaks. Or at least that's what we do where I come from."

Joel met Marcus's gaze. "It's what friends do here too."

The second knock on the front door was louder than the first. Joel tucked his pencil over his ear and stalked out to the front door. "Coming!"

Marcus stood on the other side. "You forgot about afternoon tea, didn't you?" He shook his head and walked inside. "I texted you before lunch, and never got a reply."

"Did you?" Joel had the grace to attempt a sheepish look. "Sorry, come in."

Marcus raised an eyebrow.

"Oh yeah, you're already in." Joel glanced at his watch. Three on the dot, or it would have been when Marcus had originally knocked. Joel pulled his phone from his back pocket and checked it. Three missed texts. One from Marcus, one from Darin, and another from Adelaide. "I... I, um, put it on silent so I wouldn't get disturbed."

"I hadn't noticed," Marcus said dryly. "You're at a point you can take a break, though, right?"

"Well, actually—" Joel stopped midsentence when he noticed Marcus's concerned look.

"Did you have lunch?"

"I think so." Or had that piece of toast been breakfast? "I don't remember," Joel had to admit.

"I owe Darin five dollars." Marcus sighed. "He said you'd forget to eat. I told him you'd look after yourself so you'd be able to pace yourself for the concert workload."

"Umm, sorry?" Joel would have offered to pay Darin the bet money but suspected that wouldn't go down well. "I'll go grab some shoes and my jacket. Won't be long."

Nannerl purred and rubbed around Marcus's ankles. He bent to pat her. "You need to take better care of your charge, Nannerl. Joel's your responsibility."

Joel snorted and left them to bond over his shortcomings. By the time he returned, they were nowhere to be seen. He rolled his eyes and stalked out to the kitchen in time to find Marcus spooning food into Nannerl's dish.

"She sounded hungry, and her bowl was empty. I hope that was okay."

"I fed her this morning, but it's fine. An occasional extra meal won't hurt her, but don't let her pull that one again." Joel ruffled Nannerl's fur. "That cat has you wrapped around her paw already." She always sat on Marcus's lap during Isabel's music lessons, raising her paw when he stopped petting her to signal he wasn't giving her all of the attention she deserved.

"We have an understanding." Marcus grinned and returned the rest of the cat food to the fridge. "You ready?"

"Yeah." Joel stretched, easing out the kink in his shoulders. He'd been sitting at his laptop far too long, and for an hour at the piano before that.

"Do you mind if I...?" Marcus indicated Joel's shoulders.

"That sounds wonderful." Joel turned his back to give

Marcus access. Marcus's touch was firm, his finger kneading Joel's muscles in all the right places, and his skin warm through Joel's shirt. Joel sighed, enjoying the momentary intimacy. What would Marcus's touch feel like without clothing between them? He leaned back into Marcus, relaxing for the first time all day. "You're very good at this."

Marcus stilled. "I used to do it for Garth, but he didn't enjoy it as much as you obviously are."

"Then he's an idiot." Joel didn't want to spoil the moment by discussing Marcus's ex. "That feels better, thanks." He ducked out of Marcus's reach and grabbed his jacket, which was still over the chair where he'd left it the previous morning. "Anywhere in particular you want to go?"

"We're going for lunch, or at least you are as I've had mine. I found a great place last week I'd thought you'd enjoy."

"You've been planning this a while?" Joel kept his tone casual, his mind racing with possibilities.

"It's been weeks since Oriental Bay, so yes." Marcus shrugged. "It's only a couple of blocks away so we can drive or walk. Your choice."

Joel's stomach growled. "Let's drive. We can walk another time." Presuming there would be a next time.

"Sounds good to me."

When Joel left their table and walked up to the counter to get some water, Marcus took the opportunity to study him. He had dark circles under his eyes, and he stifled a yawn. Had he worked after he'd got home last night, or hadn't he been able to sleep?

"It's nice here." Joel handed Marcus a second glass. "I'm not surprised Darin suggested it to you."

Having a café inside a gardening centre was the best of

both worlds, especially as the wind had come up while Marcus was parking the SUV.

"I had a wander around the other day." Marcus had already spotted a few plants he'd like to add to Ella's garden. "It's like being outdoors, although I'd like to try a real outside table sometime when the weather's better."

"Have you ever had an inside job, or have you always preferred to be outside?"

"I like to be outside. Inside is okay, but only in short bursts. I couldn't work in an office all day." Marcus thanked the waitress with a nod and waited for her to leave before continuing. The caramel square that accompanied his coffee looked good. Good thing they'd driven, or they would have arrived after the kitchen had closed. "Have you ever been tempted to give up teaching?"

"Sometimes, but it doesn't last long." Joel dug into his huge bowl of macaroni and cheese, waiting until he'd had a couple of mouthfuls before speaking again. "The hours are long, but I love seeing the kids get so much pleasure from music. That moment when they get lost in it, and realise they want it to be part of their life is brilliant." His face lit up, all the worry lines smoothed away by his enthusiasm. "If I can do that for only a few of them, it's still worth all the not-so-great things like all the paperwork, which I swear grows more mountainous with each year."

"I'm not a fan of paperwork either," Marcus admitted. He hadn't heard Joel play yet, but he hadn't wanted to ask as it seemed a very personal thing. And with Joel's past performance experience, it needed to be his idea. "It is a necessary evil, though. When I started out, I worked for someone whose accounting system was piles of sticky notes. It made me twitch."

"God, I couldn't deal with that." Joe shuddered. "You're enjoying working with Brendan though, yeah?"

"Yeah. He's a good guy and looking forward to cutting back his hours so he can spend more time with his wife." Marcus ate a bit of slice. "You should try some of this. It's great."

"As good as Ella's?"

"Better." Marcus glanced around in case she had any spies anywhere.

Joel laughed. "I'd be careful about her hearing that too." He took the corner that Marcus cut off for him and sighed. "I'd have to agree with you, though. This is wonderful and the chocolate on top hits the spot." He licked his lips, then swiped a bit of melted chocolate from the corner of his mouth with his tongue.

Marcus shifted in his seat, fighting the urge to lean over and clean the sliver of chocolate Joel had missed. He reached for his water and knocked it over. "Shit! Sorry."

"It's fine." Joel grabbed some napkins from a nearby table and mopped up the mess. Luckily, the glass had been almost empty.

"I'm usually not this clumsy."

"I'm sure you're not," Joel murmured. He leaned back in his chair and stretched out his shoulders.

"Still stiff?" Marcus frowned. "How long did you work this morning? Did you sleep in at least?" Not that Marcus was one for staying in bed, after years of working outdoors and wanting to make the most of the natural light.

"Nannerl wanted to go out, so I figured as I was awake already…" Joel shrugged. "I haven't been working the whole day. I sat at the piano for a couple of hours after breakfast."

"That still sounds like work." Marcus lifted Joel's bowl out of the way of the soggy napkins and placed it back in front of him. "Have you figured out what you're going to play for the concert?"

"Almost. I've narrowed it down to a couple of choices."

Joel twirled a pile of melted cheese on his fork but didn't eat it. "I need to do a lot of practise. Make sure I don't have to think when I play." His hand shook; he dropped his fork into his bowl and took a sip of water.

"You okay?" Marcus asked softly.

Joel shrugged. A determined look crossed his face. "I can't let the kids down. Some of them want to pursue their performance dreams." He blanched. "Just because mine crumpled to dust, theirs don't have to. I can't take that away from them."

"What happened?" Marcus reached across the table and placed his hand over Joel's. "You don't have to talk about it if you don't want to," he added.

"I got offered everything I wanted, and I threw it away." Joel didn't shift Marcus's hand. "Shit, I still can't think about it without…"

"I'm sorry." Marcus squeezed Joel's hand. He wished he could put his arms around Joel but wasn't sure how Joel would react.

"Thanks." Joel lowered his voice. "I found out I'd won the young performer's contest a couple of weeks before… before Darin and his family offered me a home." He didn't look at Marcus, but kept speaking in barely a whisper, the words tumbling out of him. "They didn't have a piano but that was okay. I could practise on the one at school. It was a huge thing, playing a concerto with an orchestra. I'd never done anything like that before. I walked out onto the stage, sat at the piano and…" Joel shook his head.

Marcus waited for Joel to continue in case he wanted to say more. After a couple of minutes of Joel sitting unmoving, Marcus prompted gently, "and?"

"I froze." Joel's tone turned bitter. "Couldn't bloody move. Darin had to help me off the stage and then… I threw up over him. God, I've never been so embarrassed in my life." He bit his lip. "At least I didn't have to face Dad over it and add yet another way I'd totally disappointed him."

"I'm so sorry." To hell with it. Marcus shifted his chair and put his arms around Joel. "Thank you for trusting me enough to tell me that."

"I didn't intend to." Joel leaned into Marcus's embrace, burying his head on Marcus's shoulder. "I get nervous, and I babble. You've probably noticed that less-than-wonderful attribute already."

"I kind of like it. It's genuine, like you." Marcus stopped himself from kissing the top of Joel's head.

"Hah, not sure I'd call it that." Joel pulled free of Marcus and pushed back his chair. "Let's go. I've probably already given enough of a performance for today."

"The café is almost empty." Marcus had chosen a table in the far corner away from anyone. "I doubt anyone was watching. Most people are too busy dealing with their own shit to notice anyone else's."

"Shit's a good word for it." Joel stood. "I would still like to go, if that's okay with you."

"Sure. I want to do one thing before we leave, though."

"I'll wait for you outside." Joel's expression was blank. He'd closed himself off as soon as he'd stood.

"Okay." Marcus hesitated, then decided to go ahead with what he'd planned anyway. It only took a few minutes to grab a couple more pieces of the caramel slice they'd both enjoyed. He handed Joel the paper bag when he caught up with him.

"What's this?" Joe frowned.

"Something for later." Marcus understood why Joel wanted to practise his performance piece until it was perfect, and doubted he'd be able to stop him working, but he could at least tempt him to take a break.

Joel peered inside, and his face lit up. "You... you're not... now you know what happened?"

"I don't think any the less of you if that's what you're saying." Marcus placed both hands on Joel's shoulders. "I'm sure what happened with your dad had a lot to do with what happened back then. But you're not that guy anymore. You've built a new family, and you have friends and a community who care about you. You've got this. I know you do."

CHAPTER SIX

"See you on Friday at dinner, then," Marcus said after Isabel's lesson finished. He followed Isabel down Joel's hallway but paused when he reached the front door and turned around as though he'd left something unsaid.

"Yes?" Joel asked after a few moments of awkward silence. He wrapped his fingers around the side of the door, although Marcus had his foot between it and the step to stop the open door from slamming shut in the wind.

"I... umm... I think you're a really good teacher. I enjoy bringing Isabel to her lessons." Marcus smiled, yet he seemed nervous. He leaned in closer and brushed his fingers across Joel's.

Time slowed. Joel felt his breath hitch, and he licked his lips. What would Marcus's mouth feel like pressed up against his?

Disappointment washed over him when Marcus shifted his hand higher up the door instead, glanced behind him at Isabel waiting in the SUV, and cleared his throat. "I guess I'd better get going."

"I guess so. Thanks for the compliment, though." Joel

almost asked Marcus what he was doing for dinner that night, but fortunately common sense reared its ugly head first. Ella would already have dinner ready, and her cooking was a much better option for Marcus than takeout with him. "See you Friday, then."

"Okay. Bye."

"Bye." Joel closed the door and leaned with his back against it after Marcus walked away.

They hadn't had the opportunity to talk again in private since they'd had coffee at the café a couple of weekends ago. Since his oversharing then, he'd needed to take an emotional step back. He'd deliberately been too busy to meet up with Marcus at any time when there weren't others present. Marcus seemed to have taken the hint as he'd kept busy with work, and Joel spent every spare hour preparing for the upcoming concert.

However Marcus always brought Isabel for her lessons, and they'd chat awkwardly afterwards while Isabel waited for her uncle. Conversation flowed more smoothly at the Prior's Friday night dinners. Joel made sure to keep to safe topics, and everyone chatted easily. Darin and Ella had exchanged meaningful glances from time to time, but thankfully nothing more came of it.

Joel hadn't forgotten Marcus's care, his kindness, or his acceptance of Joel, warts and all. His touch had been gentle yet strong, and Joel wondered what it would be like to kiss him. Sometimes at dinner Joel would relax and forget what had happened that day at the cafe and move closer to Marcus, who leaned in like he wanted the same thing.

Then pulled away again.

Shit. What had happened to Joel's determination to keep clear of another relationship?

Over and over, Joe took one glance at Marcus and his resolve weakened. He was very taken with Marcus's eyes. At first the colour had reminded him of clouds, but now it made him think of a coat he'd had as a child. He'd loved that coat, the warm grey offering comfort on a cold day.

Joel had rushed home from work a couple of times only to be disappointed when he found his lawns had already been mowed. He'd missed watching Marcus work. Okay, so Marcus might not take off his shirt every time he mowed the lawns, but a guy could dream, right?

Damn it. He was thinking too much.

Joel marched into the music room and pulled down a music book from the top of the piano. He flipped to the page he was looking for and started to play, the music soothing him as he lost himself in the melody. He'd finally decided which piece he wanted to play for the concert, and—

His fingers faltered on the keys when he heard a knock at the front door. Perhaps if he ignored it, whoever was disturbing him would go away. Most people would be having dinner by now, and Joel wasn't in the mood to have someone try to sell him something.

The person knocked again, this time louder.

"Bloody hell," Joel muttered. He stalked out to the front door and opened it. "Isn't it a—Marcus, what are you doing here?"

Marcus looked apologetic. "Sorry, Isabel forgot one of her music books, and she wants to practise tonight. I hope I'm not interrupting anything."

"No, it's fine. Hang on and I'll take a look." Joel didn't remember seeing anything left behind, but it never hurt to check. "Do you want to come in?"

"Sure, that way we can both look. The weather's deteriorating out there. Nasty wind coming up, and the temperature's dropped."

"Yeah, it does that." Joel walked back into the music room, knowing Marcus would follow. He glanced around, couldn't see anything, and then checked on top of the piano and by the stool. "Nothing here. Are you sure she didn't leave it in the car?"

"She seemed sure she'd left it here." Marcus glanced at the book on the piano. "Is that what you were playing before?"

"Yeah. I didn't realise you could hear it outside." Joel lifted the cushions off the sofa, shifting Nannerl in the process. The cat gave him a glare. "Nothing here either."

"You've left your front window open. Might want to shut that before it gets dark." Marcus shook his head. "I'll tell her the book isn't here. Sorry to have troubled you." He paused for a moment. "Whatever you were playing, I really liked what I could hear of it."

"Thanks," Joel mumbled. Thankfully, he was rescued from having to say anything else by Marcus's phone announcing the arrival of a text message.

Marcus fished it out of his jeans pocket and read the text aloud. "Sorry, found it."

"Isabel?" Joel asked.

"Yeah." Marcus bent to pet Nannerl. "Sorry to have bothered you. I'm sure you have stuff to do. I'll get out of your way."

"It's no trouble, really."

Ask him to stay for coffee, you idiot.

"Well, I'll see you on Friday, then."

"Yeah. Friday. Sounds good." Joel walked Marcus out to the door and watched him leave for the second time that evening.

God, could he have sounded any more pathetic? How difficult was it to ask someone to stay for coffee? He stalked into the room, shut the window, and drew the curtains, closing himself off from any distraction outside.

This time when he sat at the piano, he played scales. Up and down. Major. Minor. A third apart and then a fifth apart before moving on to arpeggios. The constant rhythm only served to fuel his frustration, and finally he slammed the lid down.

"I'm an idiot," he told Nannerl. The cat looked at him, and then jumped off the sofa and wandered towards the front door. "Great. So even you don't want to listen to me."

Joel had just reached the door to let her out when someone knocked loudly on the other side. He opened it ready to give the poor soul a piece of his mind.

"Hi, Joel." Marcus looked even more embarrassed than the last time he'd stood there. "My SUV won't start. I've rung Darin, and he suggested I wait inside for him."

"Sure, come in." Joel opened the door wider. "You're wet. I didn't realise it had started raining." Nannerl peered out the door before Joel closed it and then turned around and walked back into the living room.

"Yeah, about the same time I lifted the bonnet to see if I could figure out what was wrong with the SUV. It's hosing down out there now." Marcus shrugged off his wet coat, and Joel hung it up for him.

"I'll make some coffee," Joel offered. "Darin shouldn't be too long. Must be wet if the cat doesn't want to go out."

Marcus chuckled. "Yeah, it's raining cats and dogs out there. Thanks for the offer of the coffee. Sounds good." He followed Joel into the kitchen.

Joel put the kettle on to boil. "So," he said, suspicion starting to form in his mind. "The SUV you bought, which has been running fine, decides to suddenly not start tonight. And this is after you came back for music that Isabel didn't really leave behind?"

"Well actually it was slow turning over once about six weeks ago, but it hasn't done it again, so I didn't bother following up." Marcus perched himself on one of the barstools and leaned his elbows on the counter. "Probably should have. Hindsight and all that." His phone rang again. "It's Darin," he told Joel.

"Of course it is."

"Okay. And how long is long exactly?" Marcus glanced at Joel and rolled his eyes. "Uh-huh. So you didn't know about that job earlier, so you couldn't have swung by Joel's to pick up Isabel's music book instead of sending me out to do it?" He shook his head. "Okay, and yeah I know what serendipity means." Marcus glanced at Joel again. "Tell you what. Why don't I phone you when we're ready?" Another pause. "Because you're about as subtle as my sister and niece, that's why." He punched a button and shoved the phone back in his pocket.

"Let me guess. Darin's had something come up just as your car breaks down and strands you here."

"Yep." Marcus sounded more amused than anything. "This reminds me of when we went out for ice cream that time. I think my niece and brother-in-law have given up on their poor attempts at being subtle. I've lost track of how many times Darin's reminded me you're single, and Isabel's told me how…" He trailed off. "I hadn't told them about that afternoon a couple of a weeks ago, I swear."

"I knew you wouldn't." Joel hadn't told Marcus anything Darin didn't know already. "I made an idiot of myself that day, and I'm sorry."

"You didn't." Marcus swallowed. "Isabel has told me several times that she thinks we'd be great together. I… I didn't want another relationship."

"Neither did I," Joel added quickly, careful to use the past tense as Marcus had done. "I meant what I said about being a friend, even if I've sucked at being that too."

"You haven't. You shared a huge part of yourself, and that wouldn't have been easy. I've tried to give you some space, but I really like you, and the more I've got to know you, the more difficult it's been to keep my hands off you. I'm sorry if I've given you mixed messages." Marcus coloured and ran one hand through his hair. "I'd like to give the two of us a go if you would."

"I'd like that too, and I'm kind of guilty of giving you mixed messages too." Joel smiled. Shit. This Marcus, *awkward* Marcus, was all kinds of hot.

Marcus let out a long breath. "Great. Thing is, being with the same guy for a long time means it's been years since I've dated anyone. So I apologise up front if I suck at it."

"You and me both." Joel reached for his phone. "I haven't eaten yet, and I guess you haven't either. What say I order some pizza and call this a first date?" He grinned. "As that coffee definitely wasn't."

"Right. Pizza sounds great."

Marcus took another swig of beer and wiped his hand across his mouth. After the pizza arrived, Joel had pulled a couple of cans of beer out of the fridge. They'd decided to eat in the kitchen, and Joel shifted one of the chairs so they were sitting next to each other rather than across the table.

"I'll make some more coffee once we've finished eating," Joel said. "We can move into the living room then. It will be more comfortable."

"Thanks. I'd like that." Marcus helped himself to another slice of pizza. "The real question is whether we tell the conspirators that their plot to give us time alone together worked or keep them in the dark a while longer."

Joel laughed. The joyous sound brought a smile to Marcus's lips. "I'd say let them squirm a bit, but that depends…" Joel seemed more nervous than thoughtful.

"Depends on what?"

"On how long you want to wait." Joel shrugged. "If we're dating I won't be able to hide it. I suck at hiding my feelings, as you've probably noticed."

"That's not always a bad thing." Marcus hesitated for a moment. "I have the opposite problem. I'm not good at talking about how I feel, so I envy someone who is brave enough to voice their emotions."

"You're talking about them now." Joel bumped Marcus's shoulder, then reached across him to grab another slice of pizza.

"I figured since you did, it wasn't fair if I didn't." Marcus finished his piece of pizza. He felt comfortably full and more at ease than he had in months. Joel was easy to talk to, and when he listened, he gave the conversation his full attention. "Besides, it's not as though I don't know you. We've been chatting over dinner and after Isabel's lessons for weeks now."

"Yeah, but a lot of that was what I'd call safe conversation."

"You've said more than I have. That afternoon at the beach wasn't much but I haven't shared what I told you then with anyone else." Marcus had deliberately kept their dinner conversation light and away from anything he didn't want to talk or think about.

"We all avoid stuff we don't want to talk about. I've been told I'm really good at it." Joel visibly cringed. "God, you must have thought I was an idiot that first night at Darin's."

"You were upset about your dad." Marcus took Joel's hand and squeezed it without thinking. "If I'd found out my dad was sick, I'd be worried too."

"It wasn't just worried. I was angry." Joel glanced down at their joined hands and smiled. "I've missed being able to be with someone and talk."

"I'm sure you and Darin talk." Marcus had never met any of Joel's other friends.

"Yeah, but although we're comfortable with each other, we're not about to hold hands." Joel grinned. "Besides Darin being straight and a good friend, he's not my type."

"Not mine either." Marcus rubbed his thumb over Joel's hand. His skin felt warm, and Joel shuffled in closer. "Besides, he's married to my sister, and that would be all kinds of awkward. Not that I'd hit on him and..." Marcus didn't know why he'd felt the need to make that perfectly clear. "I don't flirt with anyone who is already taken. It's bad form."

Joel chuckled. "Your sister would kill you. She's protective as hell of the people she cares about. Although it's obvious she cares about you too, so you *might* be safe." He grew quiet and then cleared his throat. "I wouldn't do that either, though. When we first met at their wedding, I wasn't there with my partner because we were going through a rough patch. I wasn't flirting with you despite the fact I behaved like a twit."

"I noticed you at the wedding too. I thought you were cute." Marcus shrugged. "I didn't think you behaved like a twit. It was an awkward moment, and Garth probably didn't help."

"That guy was your ex? Short, red hair, and glasses?"

"Yeah. He never liked it when I talked to cute guys. We hadn't been together long, which probably didn't help."

"Cute?" Joel stuck his lower lip out in a pout. "Not hot? Just cute?"

Marcus chuckled at the obviously fake pout. He brushed a lock of hair away that had fallen across Joel's face and leaned in closer. "I remember cute. I happen to like cute guys. I think they're hot. Or they can be." His heart sped up. Did he dare to...?

Joel met Marcus's gaze for a long moment before turning away. "Why don't I put the kettle on again, and we can move into the living room?"

"Okay." Marcus felt a surge of disappointment wash over him. This was a first date despite the number of times they'd seen each other before tonight. Joel might be one of those guys who only talked on first dates. Not that Marcus was one to do much more, but... He'd waited this long to be more than friends with Joel. A bit longer wouldn't kill him.

So much for spending the past few weeks trying to convince himself he didn't want a relationship. He'd had feelings for Joel for much longer than he'd wanted to admit, and spent the night after the wet t-shirt episode having the type of dreams a guy definitely didn't have about someone he considered just a friend. He'd worn a smile at breakfast the following morning that resulted in several grins from the rest of his family.

God, had he been that obvious?

Apparently so, if Isabel's pretence of leaving her music at Joel's—and then Darin conveniently being too busy to pick him up—were anything to go by.

"I can hear you thinking from here." Joel turned the kettle on and retrieved a couple of clean cups from the dishwasher. "I... Don't worry, I won't pry. Although I tend to not know when to shut up, I don't expect you to be the same."

"I don't expect you to be the same as me either." Marcus decided it was time to change the subject. "How's the planning for the concert going? You've started rehearsals, right?"

"Yeah, we started as soon as I got the music organised. It's going okay. One of the pieces ended up being too much of a challenge, so I swapped it out for something else. Sometimes it's difficult to find that fine line between too easy and too difficult. I have a friend who conducts a local community orchestra for kids. She's given me some ideas and can loan me the music too, which will save time."

"It still sounds like a lot of work."

"Yeah, well." Joel shrugged. "I kind of like it that way."

He poured their coffee, handed Marcus a cup, and led the way to the living room. Marcus glanced around curiously. He hadn't seen inside Joel's living room before, as the door was usually closed when he passed it on his way to the spare bedroom Joel had converted into a music room. A large TV took up one corner, the shelves on either side lined with DVDs. A closer look revealed a stereo system with a turntable tucked between the TV and one of the shelves—which was full of CDs, not DVDs as Marcus had first thought. The shelf below it had an impressive collection of vinyl. Bookcases stood side by side on another wall, crammed full of books in a variety of different genres. Marcus spotted a few of his favourite authors, and others he'd never heard of. He'd have to ask Joel if he could borrow some books.

Two comfortable sofas took up the rest of the room with a wooden coffee table between them. Joel flopped down on one end of the loveseat. "The concert's taking most of my free time, though, so… we're going to have to find a way around it if we're going to give dating a go."

"We'll find a way around it." Marcus took the other end of the same sofa, rather than the empty three-seater. "I'm flexible, if you are."

Joel grinned. "I'm sure you are." He took a sip of his coffee.

"If your rehearsals go late after school, I could pick you up for dinner afterwards, unless you prefer that I wait till you get home. "Either works." Was Joel out about his sexuality at school?

"Sure. You could come by the school a bit earlier if you

wanted to listen to some of the rehearsal. The choir practises on Mondays, and orchestra is on Wednesdays, so either of those is a good evening to go out if we're not too late. I'll need some time off after rehearsal anyway."

"Yeah, sounds good." Marcus stretched his legs out in front of him. Outside the wind had died down, although he could still hear the steady beat of rain on the roof. He stifled a yawn. "Sorry, it's not the conversation. It's been a long day."

"I haven't asked how your job is going. Sorry."

"No need to apologise. I asked you about school and I like listening to you talk about it." Marcus never wanted Joel to think he couldn't talk as much as he needed to. "And although I don't know much about music, it doesn't mean I don't enjoy listening to it." He studied his cup, deciding where to start. "The job's going well. Working with someone else has taken a bit of getting used to as I worked alone and was my own boss for years. Brendan's very easy-going, though, and leaves me to get on with it. We're still working on how we're going to get more clients for the other side of the business—things we can do in any weather. As much as it rains around here, we need to diversify, or we'll spend most of the winter sitting on our hands."

"You need some downtime." Joel conveniently forgot he taught two evenings a week, took choir and orchestra rehearsals on two of the other days, and fitted in lesson prep and marking around all of it.

"Yes, but I prefer to keep busy. I start getting twitchy otherwise."

"I'm sure I could help with that." Joel grinned.

"I thought you wanted to take things slow and see where they might lead," Marcus murmured. He shifted in his seat, his cock helpfully reminding him that his hormones weren't exactly agreeing with his words.

"Yeah, I do. Sorry." Joel shrugged. "I told you I talk too much. I guess I've... Never mind."

"It's fine. You're putting into words the stuff I'm not saying." Marcus studied his coffee, blew on it to cool it a bit, and then took a decent-sized drink of it. "I was kind of hoping you might play for me whatever it was I interrupted when I arrived. The first time this evening, that is."

"The second time," Joel corrected absently. "The first time you came with Isabel."

Marcus put his cup down on the coffee table. "Was that a yes, I will, or no, I won't?" He hesitated. "If you don't want to, I understand."

"Oh, sorry." Joel set his cup next to Marcus's. "My coffee's still a bit warm. I can play for you now if you want, and then we can finish our drinks." He smiled. "And it's fine. I'm okay with a small audience, or as long as I'm not the centre of attention. Otherwise I wouldn't be able to accompany the choir at school. What time do you need to leave?"

Marcus checked his watch and was surprised by how late it was. "I'd better phone Darin soon, I guess. I have an early start tomorrow."

"Yeah, me too." Joel slipped his hand into Marcus's and led him down the hallway to the music room.

"Want me to take my usual spot?" Marcus didn't want to distract Joel too much.

"Yeah, if that works. Sorry, there isn't another sofa in the room. I've never had a need for it." Joel settled himself down on the piano stool and opened the lid.

Marcus hadn't noticed how sparsely furnished the room was. Apart from the piano and the small table and chair next to it, there was only one sofa and a bookcase full of sheet music in the corner.

"That works."

Nannerl pushed past Marcus and jumped up onto the sofa, sprawling out to take up the entire seat.

"Or not," Marcus said. "I'll take your usual seat."

"You can shift her, you know." Joel glanced at Nannerl. "I swear that cat has a mind of her own."

"She's a cat, and your chair looks comfortable enough. Besides, I can see better from here." Marcus pushed the chair back, stretched his legs out, and crossed them at the ankles. "What's the music?" Not that it would mean much to him, but he wanted to be able to put a name to it.

"It's a Chopin prelude. I've always liked playing Chopin. I find it relaxing, as it's easy to lose myself in the music. I'm hoping that helps me not to stress out too much on the night of the concert." Joel adjusted the distance between the stool and the piano and then began to play.

Marcus nodded. He'd heard of Chopin—Joel had mentioned his music before.

Despite his intention to watch Joel play, Marcus closed his eyes. It felt as though Joel projected some of himself into his performance. Nuances of emotion reached out to Marcus as the melody grew louder, in both volume and intensity, and faster. Then slower again, the melody taking centre stage, with a repeating deeper note before the music finished.

"Wow." Marcus opened his eyes.

Joel still sat poised at the keyboard. He placed his hands on his lap, interlacing his fingers, his knuckles white. "Wow? Really? I need to practise more, and that bit with the—"

Marcus didn't have the words to describe what he'd heard. He'd liked it. A lot. Not just for the music but the insight it gave him into Joel. He leaned over, gently brushed his fingers against Joel's face, and when Joel turned to face him, Marcus kissed him on the lips. Softly at first, then deepening as Joel threaded his fingers through Marcus's hair and pulled him closer.

When Joel caressed Marcus's lips with his tongue, Marcus groaned. Why had he waited so long for this? Kissing Joel felt right—as though he'd found something he'd never known was missing.

When they finally broke the kiss, Joel leaned his forehead against Marcus's. "Wow," he whispered. "I should play for you more often."

"Yes," Marcus said. "I think you should." He reached for Joel's shirt and began undoing the buttons. "Yes?"

"Yes. Definitely yes." Joel yanked Marcus's T-shirt over his head. "Hot," he murmured, then shoved the stool back further and stood at the same time Marcus did. "I've wanted to do this since that first day you mowed my lawns."

"Shit." Marcus half gasped, half groaned when Joel flicked his nipples with his tongue. He rubbed himself up against Joel. Joel was as hard as Marcus.

"Bedroom. Now," Joel whispered.

Marcus nodded, his mouth dry. To hell with waiting. The kiss had opened a floodgate of desire he didn't want to end. Now that they'd decided to go for this, he didn't see any reason to stop.

Someone knocked loudly on the front door.

"You have *got* to be kidding me," Joel said.

The knocking grew more insistent.

"Bloody hell," Marcus muttered. "Whoever this is, it had better be good." He flopped down on the sofa. Nannerl scooted to one side to avoid him. "You'd better get it. Might be someone important."

He'd never forgive himself if it was one of Joel's family and something had happened to his father. He took several deep breaths. He and Joel wanted to be together. A few more minutes waiting wouldn't hurt.

"It had better be." Joel shrugged on his shirt and stomped out to the front door.

Marcus heard a familiar voice and groaned aloud. "Bloody hell," he muttered again. Not bothering to pull on his T-shirt, he strode out of the room.

Darin took one glance at him and looked guilty as hell. As he should be. "Sorry," he mumbled. "At least I knocked instead of using my key."

"I told you I'd phone." Marcus stood behind Joel and slid his arms around him.

"That job turned out to be bigger than I expected, and I'll have to finish it early tomorrow morning, so…" He looked at Marcus and Joel. "I should have left it a bit longer, right?"

"Yeah." Marcus sighed. "Rain check," he whispered in Joel's ear.

"Oh, yeah." Joel turned and brushed his lips across Marcus's cheek, apparently not worried they had an audience. He then cleared his throat and spoke to Darin. "You'd better come in."

CHAPTER SEVEN

"Thanks for the ride," Marcus said.

"It's the least I could do." Darin had apologised most of the way home the night before. "I was going to wait for you to call me last night, honest."

"Yeah, you've told me that already."

As much as Marcus was tempted to hold it over Darin, he couldn't bring himself to do so. After all, Darin was partly the reason Marcus and Joel had finally told each other how they felt. Marcus loved the feel of Joel's lips against his own and the sweet yet sexy kiss that promised so much more.

"And I'll fix your SUV free of charge. With a new starter motor, it shouldn't give you any more problems." Darin shrugged. "As I already told you, last night was pure serendipity. You guys are meant to be together. Even the universe agrees."

"You don't need to repeat all this stuff. And I'll pay you for your labour as well as the part. It's the least I can do. After all, you did convince Issy to hold off texting me to say she'd found her music."

Darin rolled his eyes. "I still can't believe you were going to leave before your SUV broke down. You guys are as bad as each other."

"So, you would have tried convincing Joel to make a move if this hadn't worked?"

"Well, duh." Darin grinned, apparently having reached his quota of grovelling. "Ella said you sometimes need a couple of shoves in the right direction, and who am I to argue with my beautiful wife? You guys were never going to get any time alone unless you had a reason to go around there when Joel had no students. It was the perfect opportunity."

"Sure. Whatever." Marcus shrugged. "It's done." He paused. "But if you interrupt us again this evening, I won't be so forgiving. Once is an accident… twice—"

"I held off as long as I could, but a leaky hose turned into a radiator replacement, and he's a regular customer and in a tight spot so…"

Marcus had felt a minute degree of satisfaction that Darin's brilliant plan had backfired on him. It took the edge off his annoyance at having his time with Joel interrupted. He climbed out of the truck, shut the door, and turned to face Darin through the open window. "I need to go. Don't wait up. I'll see you when I see you."

"Enjoy your evening." Darin winked, waved, and pulled out into the traffic.

"Thanks. I intend to." Marcus figured it was easier to get dropped off at the school, as Joel had offered to take Marcus back to Darin's at the end of the evening.

Or not.

Joel had given Marcus directions to the auditorium where the orchestra rehearsals took place. He'd told Marcus that they usually practised in a classroom, but he'd figured it was better if the orchestra got used to the acoustics of the performance venue. Despite Marcus's intentions to be there earlier, fate had conspired against him. First his job had taken longer than he'd anticipated, then Darin got held up too.

Hopefully, Marcus would catch the last twenty minutes or so of the rehearsal, but when he'd texted Joel about being late, he hadn't received a reply. He mentally crossed his fingers that meant Joel was too busy to check his phone, rather than annoyed that Marcus was late. As though on cue, his phone alerted him to a text. He swiped the screen and shook his head.

Bloody hell, Garth. Marcus had texted him back a few times reminding him they were done and hadn't heard anything from him for a few weeks. He'd hoped Garth had finally given up. But he'd always been determined when he went after something or someone he wanted. It appeared this was no exception.

Marcus shoved the phone back into his pocket and poked his head into the school office. The older woman working there was packing up, ready to go home. Joel had told Marcus to introduce himself so the school would know he wasn't some random stranger wandering around.

"Hi, I'm Marcus Verden. Joel's expecting me." When his comment was met with a frown, he added as part of his introduction, "Isabel Prior's my niece. My sister, Ella, said she was going to talk to you about adding me to Isabel's emergency contact list."

"Right. Of course." The woman nodded. "Hello, Mr Verden. I'm Nancy Cahill. I remember Isabel talking about you. She's not part of the orchestra, though."

"Yeah, I know. As I said, I'm meeting Joel. Mr Ashcroft." Marcus wished Joel had told him whether he was out at school or not. Being able to introduce himself as Joel's boyfriend would make this a lot easier. "I'm a friend," he said finally. "And nice to meet you… Ms Cahill." He didn't want to be obviously looking to see if she was wearing a wedding ring, so wasn't sure what honorific to use, but Ms was usually a safe bet.

"Ah, okay, it's always nice to meet a friend of Joel's." Nancy smiled widely. "My wife is a musician. She and Joel have known each other for years." She pointed to a corridor on her right. "You'll find Joel in the auditorium at the end of that corridor. The orchestra's sounding great. He's doing an amazing job with those kids."

"Thanks." Marcus ignored the group of teenage girls watching him and decided not to ponder about how much of the conversation they'd heard. Instead he headed off in the direction she'd indicated and soon found himself in front of two sets of closed double doors. He opened one of them and slipped inside.

Joel stood on the stage at the front of the orchestra. When the door opened, he looked up and smiled.

Several of the kids in the orchestra turned around to see what Joel was looking at. A couple of the girls sitting in the front row of violins glanced back at Joel and then again at Marcus, but they didn't say anything.

Joel cleared his throat. "Okay, let's take that one from bar thirty. Everyone found that? It's two before the first-time bar, so we're going to play from there and do the repeat. I'll give you a bar for nothing." He raised his baton. "One. Two. Three."

The orchestra began playing one of the tunes Joel had been humming at dinner the week before. Marcus found a seat at the front of the hall next to a woman about his own age. She tapped her foot along with the music and kept her eyes on Joel more closely than the musicians did.

A few other adults sat around them, listening. One woman seemed absorbed in whatever was on her tablet, although she nodded in time with the music and looked up when the flutes began to play.

Probably parents come to pick up their kids.

Marcus suddenly felt the odd one out, although he didn't regret coming. Joel had an intensity about him when he conducted that was missing when he gave piano lessons. Although he'd been focused on his students then too, this felt different. Conducting was something Joel clearly loved—it reminded Marcus of when Joel had played the prelude for him.

A trumpet blared, jarring Marcus from his thoughts.

Joel lowered his baton, and although most of the orchestra stopped, the kid playing the trumpet didn't seem to notice.

"Quentin!" Joel called, and the kid suddenly stopped playing.

"Yes, Mr Ashcroft?"

"I think you're a couple of bars ahead of the rest of us. You're sounding great, but it doesn't quite work if you come in at the wrong place." Joel spoke softly, so it didn't sound like a reprimand.

One of the boys playing clarinet grinned, and the girl next to him giggled.

"Everyone makes mistakes," Joel said. "Next time it might be someone else coming in at the wrong place. Even me."

The whole orchestra laughed.

"Now, I think we can run this through from where we were before, but this time we'll ignore the repeat and keep going until the end of the piece. So play the second-time bar instead of the first. Okay?"

"Okay, Mr Ashcroft," the kids chorused.

"Joel's so very good with the students, don't you think?" the woman next to Marcus whispered.

It took him a moment to realise she was talking to him.

"Oh, yes. He's very good with them." Marcus took care to keep his voice low so he wouldn't disturb the rehearsal.

"This is your first time here, isn't it?" The woman twirled a strand of blonde hair with one finger. "I'm Adelaide Barker. I'm here on behalf of the PTA. This concert was my idea, you know. I think Joel is so talented."

Ah so she was *that* Adelaide Barker. He doubted there would be more than one, considering the way both Ella and Joel spoke of her.

"He's very talented." Marcus turned his attention back to Joel. He'd seen an echo of that expression on Joel's face when they'd kissed. Joel had been right when he said he didn't hide his emotions, but Marcus liked that. Joel had responded so eagerly to his touch, and the feel of his bare skin against Marcus's had left Marcus craving more. He couldn't wait to continue from where they'd left off. He'd dreamed of Joel that night and woken to his heart racing and a hard-as-hell erection. Fuck, if jacking off in the shower thinking about Joel felt so good, he couldn't wait for the real thing.

"So which child is yours, Mr...?" Adelaide interrupted Marcus's thoughts.

Marcus flushed. This wasn't the place to be thinking about how being with Joel made him feel. He mumbled a quick reply. "My niece is at the school."

Adelaide studied him. "I knew you looked familiar, but I couldn't place it. You're Ella Prior's brother, aren't you? She mentioned something about you moving up here. I can see some of your sister and your niece in you. Mark, isn't it?"

"Marcus," Marcus corrected. Her conversation was beginning to irritate him. Not only that, but he was trying to listen to the music. He shot her a glare without thinking.

"I'm only trying to be friendly," she huffed. "And besides, Isabel's not in the orchestra. She plays piano. Like my Caleb. My Caleb's very good, you know. Joel's such a great teacher."

Luckily at that point Joel lowered his baton again, and the orchestra stopped playing. "That's it for this week, guys. Big improvement from last week, so all your hard work is paying off. Same time next week, okay? We'll be rehearsing the Anderson and the Strauss. Don't forget to practise. See you next week."

As the orchestra began to pack up, Joel sprinted down the stairs and walked over to Marcus. "You made it."

"Yeah. I thought the orchestra sounded good. Really good." Marcus ducked his head. "Not that I'd know, but it sounded good to me."

"Thanks. I chose music I hoped would be enjoyed by everyone, not only musicians, so knowing you liked it means a lot." Joel smiled, his eyes lighting up. "We still need to do a bit of work, but it's getting there. I need to pack up first. Hope you don't mind waiting."

"I can give you a hand if you point me in the right direction."

Adelaide bristled by Marcus's side. She coughed loudly. "Why don't you let me help Joel pack up? After all, I'm sure you have somewhere you need to be as Isabel has left for the day. It's understandable that you'd want a sneak preview of the concert, but you know it's a fundraiser, so you'll have to wait to pay to hear it like everyone else."

Joel let out a frustrated sigh. "Mrs Barker—"

"Adelaide, please. After all, we've known each other a while." Adelaide shot Marcus a glare that clearly said she didn't appreciate him hanging around a rehearsal he had no business being at.

Marcus slid his arm around Joel's waist. "I think there's been a misunderstanding, Mrs Barker," he said quickly. "I'm not here to get a sneak preview of the concert. I've come to pick Joel up for dinner."

Adelaide's mouth dropped open.

"Oh, didn't I mention that, Adelaide?" Joel snaked his right arm behind him, caught Marcus's hand, and squeezed it. Joel gave her an innocent look Marcus didn't believe for a second. "I'm sorry. That was rude of me. I should have introduced Marcus properly when we started talking. Adelaide Barker, this is Marcus Verden. Marcus, Mrs Barker." Joel paused for a moment, although it was obvious Adelaide had already connected the dots. "He's my boyfriend."

∾

"I hope you didn't mind me outing you." Marcus slid the last pile of chairs into the storage room off the hall and pulled down the roller door. "I thought... I wasn't sure if you were out at school, but that woman—"

"Means well but can be bloody annoying." Joel glanced around to make sure they were alone. The kids had helped put the equipment away, but Joel sensed some of the parents getting impatient so he'd thanked them and told them he could finish up.

"That's one way of putting it." Marcus pulled Joel into his arms and kissed him. "I did out you, didn't I?" he whispered after they broke the kiss.

"Yeah, but it's not exactly a big secret. And I was the one who told her you were my boyfriend." Joel shrugged. He'd only told Adelaide what she would have already worked out by then. She'd mumbled a hasty goodbye and taken off shortly afterwards. "Most of the other teachers know, but I don't broadcast it. I've never had a reason to."

"Not even for Reed?" Marcus raised an eyebrow.

"I'd only just started here before we broke up, and he never really dropped by the school, as he usually worked later than I did. At my last school whenever we had staff social events, he tended to have stuff on." Joel had never felt the need to introduce Reed to his friends at this school either. And then after they'd broken up, he was pleased he hadn't; it was less awkward that way. "And then there's Mrs Barker."

"I'm guessing whoever didn't know that you're gay and have a boyfriend *will* know by tomorrow."

"Tomorrow? It will be well done and dusted by then." Joel shrugged again. Adelaide Barker been the main reason he'd never officially come out at school. "I swear she's the modern equivalent of an old-fashioned village gossip." He grinned. The expression on her face when she'd figured out who Marcus was had been priceless. He'd be replaying that moment in his mind for weeks to come, if not longer.

"I didn't like the way she looked at you," Marcus said. "She kept going on about how fabulous you are, and although I know that, I didn't… God, I hope that doesn't make me sound like a possessive idiot. That's the last thing I want, or you need."

"It doesn't make you sound like that at all." Joel hunted for the right words. "I'd be annoyed if she'd gone on about you that way too." He brushed his fingers across Marcus's cheek. Damn Darin and his timing from hell the other night. "You were making it clear I'm spoken for. I think it's hot." He had a visual of Marcus as a knight in shining armour and let out a loud sigh. "Fucking hot."

"You are spoken for—at least if you want to be." Marcus leaned into Joel's touch. "We should get out of here. Just because we're alone for now doesn't mean we won't get interrupted, and there will be enough gossip going on without adding fuel to the fire."

"Yeah, sure. Add to the knight in shining armour image," Joel murmured, trying not to laugh at the idea of Adelaide as the resident dragon. "Don't ask," he said when Marcus looked puzzled. "I need to grab my stuff from my classroom, and then we can head out." Joel locked the hall, then ducked into the office to hang up the keys. "You got dropped off, right?"

"Right." Marcus followed Joel up the stairs. "Adelaide isn't the only one who will talk. A couple of the girls were whispering and giggling. I think they figured it out."

"Yeah, well, I thought as much." Joel hadn't noticed, but it didn't take a genius to work out who those girls were. "Don't worry. I can deal with it."

"I wouldn't have risked outing you otherwise." Marcus leaned against the classroom wall while he waited for Joel to collect his bag.

"It's done now, and I'd prefer to focus on this evening." Joel brushed his hand against Marcus's arm. "I hope Darin was thoroughly contrite when he dropped you off."

"I think he got the message when you kissed me in front of him." Marcus grinned—a smug almost-smirk that reminded Joel of a satisfied cat.

"Keep that expression and we won't be able to leave this classroom," he murmured.

"Don't worry. I can repeat it later." Marcus winked. He laughed. "It's ironic. After all Darin's planning with Isabel to ensure we had time alone so we'd make a move on each other, when we do, he interrupts us. He muttered a few things on the way home, and I don't think I've ever heard him apologise so many times about one thing."

"I bet." Joel rolled his eyes. "Serves him right, although—" He kissed Marcus softly on the lips. "—we should be thanking him, really."

"Yeah, we should, but don't tell him that. At least not yet."

"I think we should get home." Joel grabbed Marcus's hand and headed for the door. "Question is, though, collect takeout first or order in afterwards?" One look confirmed that Marcus wanted to pick up where they'd left off as badly as Joel did.

Any interruptions tonight would be ignored.

And sworn at.

Marcus hesitated. "As much as I don't want to wait, I vote for getting something on the way home. Once we start, I don't want to stop, and I don't know about you, but I'm hungry."

"Me too." Joel wasn't just talking about food, and he didn't think Marcus was either. "There's a Chinese takeout on High Street. Work for you?" That way if they changed their minds, they'd have food they could reheat for later.

"Oh, yeah," Marcus replied as they reached the bottom of the stairs. He licked his lips. "As I said, I'm hungry."

"Hmmm." Joel fumbled in his pocket for his keys when they reached the car park, then jabbed at the button to unlock the car. As soon as Marcus was settled in the passenger seat, Joel turned the key and the stereo blared into life. He'd forgotten he'd turned up the volume on his CD that morning.

"Not classical music?" Marcus raised an eyebrow as "Dominion Road" by the Mutton Birds started to play.

"I don't only listen to classical music," Joel said indignantly. "And besides, I like the Mutton Birds. Don McGlashan's solo stuff is good too."

"They do a decent cover of 'Don't Fear the Reaper.'" Marcus laughed at Joel's surprised look. "Hey, just because I said I don't know much about music doesn't mean I don't listen to it at all. Besides, it's on the soundtrack for *The Frighteners*, and I like that movie."

"So do I, and I have a copy of it if you'd like to rewatch sometime. Darin's dad introduced us both to it; it's one of his favourites."

"Sounds great. My dad loves it too." Marcus opened the glove box when Joel motioned towards it, and read the names of the tracks on the CD. "I didn't realise they had a greatest hits CD out."

Joel laughed. "It came out years ago, so I've had it a while. I have a decent selection of New Zealand music. I like to support our local musicians, and besides, they were damn good."

"I haven't heard a lot. You can educate me." Marcus put the CD cover away and closed the glove box. "I didn't have much of a collection and the few I had I left behind, so I tend to play the radio when I'm driving. The stereo in my SUV is older, so I don't have a lot of options."

"I've never got around to updating this one either although I could plug my phone in if I wanted to," Joel admitted. "I have a lot of stuff on CDs, though, so there's no rush. You can borrow some of mine if you want.

"Thanks, I might do that." "Anchor Me" started to play, and Marcus frowned. "I'm sure that wasn't the next track on the CD."

"It's on shuffle," Joel explained as he pulled up in front of the takeaway. "I don't always want to know what to expect in life." He'd found it was easier that way. After Reed left, Joel had discovered how much of a routine he'd been living in and decided he wasn't going to fall into that trap again. Some things he couldn't change, but having his CD player on shuffle... He saw Marcus's shoulders stiffen slightly. "You don't agree?"

"I..." Marcus looked away. "I'm more comfortable knowing what's coming, although..." He sighed. "I thought I had my life all mapped out, you know. Garth and I were going to grow old together. He had his farm, and I had my business, and I thought we were happy. And I was, for the first few years we were together, but—" He stopped midsentence and shrugged.

"Maybe he wasn't the right person for you," Joel said

softly. That answered his question as to whether Marcus had left his ex or vice versa. "I'm sorry. Breaking up isn't easy, even when it's your decision."

"I gave the relationship a decent go before I left, even warned him a few times that I'd had enough of his bullshit. He'd apologise but any change in behaviour only lasted a few weeks. It wasn't as though ending it should have come as a huge surprise to him."

"My ex—Reed—wanted me to go to Australia with him. I didn't." Joel didn't think it was fair that Marcus was the only one baring his soul. He turned off the ignition, and the music cut off midsong.

"I'm glad you decided to stay," Marcus said softly. "Not that you went through breaking up with him, though. I wouldn't wish that on anyone."

"Neither would I." Joel caressed Marcus's cheek, and Marcus turned to meet his gaze. "I know we both said we'd hesitated over doing anything because of Darin and how awkward it would be if it ended badly, but it wasn't just because of that." Better to say this now and get it over with. "I parted ways with Reed five years ago, but sometimes it feels like yesterday. I wasn't in a hurry to go through that again."

"Six months for me." Marcus leaned into Joel's touch and grew silent. Finally he placed his hand over Joel's, slid their joined hands from his face, and stroked his thumb against Joel's fingers. "I've spent too much of my life being predictable, and then I met you, and you have a fire about you I haven't seen in a very long time."

"I've been grumpy as hell and on a downer for the past few months," Joel protested.

"You're honest about how you feel," Marcus said, "and as I've told you, I like that. I always thought Garth was too much like me, but he never would have broken up with me however bad things got between us."

"If what you just told me isn't being honest, I don't know what is." Joel glanced at the shop full of people. "Tell you what. I vote for changing our minds and going straight home. I have stuff in the fridge, and I'll cook a meal for us later. I'd like an evening of just us, starting now." He leaned over and kissed Marcus, putting all the desire he could into the kiss. "I want you, to touch you with nothing between us. Nothing at all."

Marcus growled low in his throat. "I'm still hungry, but not for dinner. That can wait. I want you too."

∾

Joel slammed his front door behind them and dropped his keys on the floor. He licked his lips and looked Marcus up and down. "That was the longest drive home, ever." His eyes darkened.

"You barely stayed under the speed limit." Marcus pulled Joel close and kissed him hard. He'd briefly rested his hand on Joel's thigh after they'd climbed back into the car, then removed it when Joel's breathing had sped up so he could focus on the road.

Joel broke the kiss. "Yeah well, patience isn't one of my strengths." He yanked at the bottom of Marcus's jersey, his eyes widening. "Fuck, how many layers do you have on under that?"

"I feel the cold." Marcus shivered as he dragged his T-shirt and singlet up over his head with his jersey, although it had nothing to do with the temperature.

Joel gripped the waistband of Marcus's jeans with one hand, then bent his head, and flicked his tongue over Marcus's already hardened nipples.

God, Joel's tongue felt good. Marcus's cock hardened, and he groaned. "Bedroom," he ground out.

Joel pushed Marcus against the wall and kissed him again. He rubbed his cock against Marcus's, both their erections straining against their jeans. Joel took a tiny step back so he could slide his hand between them, undid the top button of Marcus's jeans, and ran his fingers through the trail of hair leading to his cock.

Marcus grabbed Joel's buttocks and pulled him close, closing the gap between them. "Bedroom first." He wasn't going to have their first time in a hallway. And sure as hell not until Joel had shed some clothing.

"Bossy." Joel nipped Marcus's earlobe. He sucked on the skin, his breath warm against Marcus's face. "I want to do so much with you. Touch *everything*." His voice grew husky. "Play you like… shit." Joel groaned.

"Fuck, yes." The thought of Joel's fingers on him like he'd caressed the keys on his piano sent heat through Marcus. His balls tightened. He took a deep breath.

Marcus pushed out from the wall, taking Joel with him. He glanced down the hallway. Which door led to the bedroom?

Joel grinned and crooked his finger. Marcus followed, catching up to Joel at the doorway. He caressed Joel's firm arse and yanked his t-shirt free of his jeans. Joel opened the door, shrugged off his t-shirt, and threw it on the floor. He turned to look at Marcus and swallowed.

"You're gorgeous," he whispered.

"So are you."

Dark hair covered Joel's chest between his nipples and downwards. Marcus couldn't tear his gaze away from the tantalising trail, and then he watched, mouth dry, while Joel undid his jeans and shoved them down to pool at his feet.

His cotton boxers clung to him, his cock alert and leaking precum.

Marcus's breath hitched. "Wow." He shoved his jeans off and kicked them to one side.

Joel's eyes widened. "Definitely wow." He licked his lips, shoved down his boxers, and swallowed. Hard. "I want you. Now."

Marcus got rid of his boxers and closed the short distance between them. He caught Joel in a searing kiss, rubbing their cocks together. Joel backed them towards the bed, then lay down, puling Marcus on top of him. Their kisses grew more desperate. Joel squeezed Marcus's buttocks and writhed under him.

"Bloody hell." Marcus forced himself to stop, and shifted so he was crouched over Joel, his cock dangling over his stomach. Marcus was hard as hell.

Joel slid his hand between them, stroking Marcus's cock. He rolled them so they were facing sideways.

"Condom?"

"Not going to get that far. Next time." Joel sped up his strokes, his fingers dancing a rhythm up and down Marcus's length.

Heat built between them. Marcus groaned again. He rolled them so he was on top, rubbing frantically against Joel. Joel kissed him, his tongue mirroring the frantic pace as they moved against each other.

Marcus's vision went white. He cried out, clinging to Joel, kissing him over and over. "Oh… bloody hell. Fuck."

"Marcus!" Joel wrapped his legs around Marcus, holding him close as they both shuddered and came.

Marcus panted, shivering, clinging to Joel. He kissed his face, then down his shoulder. "I've never… oh God." He collapsed, his softening cock twitching. He'd never had sex like that before. Ever. "You're amazing."

"You're not so bad yourself." Joel caressed Marcus's cheek. He kissed him gently on the lips, taking his time as though savouring something precious. "Let's lie here a while, hmm? I want you in my arms."

"I'd like that too." Marcus managed a shaky smile. "I... I brought stuff with me. In case."

Joel laughed. "Like a boy scout, hmm?" He grinned. "Dinner, then—"

"Round two?" Marcus kissed up Joel's jaw. "And this time I want you in me... unless—" He wouldn't presume. Everything they did had to be because they both wanted it. "I... I'm happy either way."

"So am I, and I'd like that." Joel tilted his head back and twisted his fingers through Marcus's hair. "You in me, I mean. I'd like it a lot."

CHAPTER EIGHT

Marcus woke early the next morning to a comfortable realisation he wasn't alone—and that Joel was the warm body in bed with him. Marcus had wrapped his arm around Joel at some point in the night, so he disentangled himself, careful not to wake him.

Sunlight peeked through the gap at the top of the curtains, giving the room a warm glow. Joel looked so peaceful, almost angelic, although that definitely was not a description that suited him. Not considering the amazing sex they'd had the night before.

Wow.

Joel had teased Marcus right to the edge and then taken them both over it. And the look in Joel's eyes—passion and need all rolled into one very sexy package. Marcus loved the way Joel made him feel complete. Marcus had seen an echo of his emotions in Joel when he had explored Joel's body in turn. Joel responded to every touch, his breath hitching, his voice an almost growl as he demanded Marcus give him what he needed. "Take me," he'd said. "Take me now!"

They'd sped up, then taken their time enjoying each other

before finishing with a final round of fast and needy. By the time they were done, Marcus hadn't been able to think straight, and then he'd settled into a warm afterglow, smiling.

He hadn't felt this sated in… forever. Sex with Joel wasn't simply a physical act; it had seeped into Marcus's core and embraced his emotions too.

While he'd enjoyed the physical part of his relationship with Garth, being with Joel felt different. It touched Marcus deep down, and—although he usually wasn't one for thinking poetically—he could have sworn for one brief moment his world had dissolved, leaving him and Joel together, and nothing else.

Joel mumbled something in his sleep. A stray lock of hair moved in time with his breathing, back and forth, brushing against his forehead. Marcus tucked it behind Joel's ear, not wanting him to wake yet. Their workday would begin soon enough, as they both had early starts that morning, but the alarm wouldn't sound and shatter this glimpse of a possible new reality for another few minutes. Marcus needed to remember the intimacy of being with Joel, although he hoped like hell their first time together was the beginning of many more.

He longed to have Joel in his life. More than he'd realised. Despite their different backgrounds, they fit together, not only physically but emotionally too. Joel had reignited the passion Marcus used to have years ago, before he'd grown used to the stagnant life he'd once thought enough. In return for that gift of passion, Marcus would be there for Joel, to support him when things got rough, and to offer calm in whatever storm came his way.

He wasn't just falling for Joel, he'd plunged headfirst. Why had he waited?

Oh, yeah, because if this went to hell in a handbasket, it was going to be awkward as. He'd once vowed he'd never get involved with someone connected to family, but that had gone out the window—so quickly it almost scared him—when he'd fallen for Joel.

Loud purring interrupted his thoughts. Nannerl jumped onto the bed and squeezed between Marcus and Joel. She looked at Joel and then Marcus, before settling down between them as though finding the two of them in bed together was totally normal.

Marcus smiled. He yearned for starting each day with Joel in their bed so much.

"Wanna sleep. Go away, cat." Joel mumbled.

Marcus reached over and switched off the alarm. He captured Joel's mouth in a deep kiss as Joel opened his eyes.

"Hmm, I could get used to waking up like this." Joel smiled, then glanced between them. "Bloody cat. I swear she thinks this bed is hers. Shift her if you want."

"It's fine." Marcus had no intention of letting a cat overturn anything he and Joel chose to do. "I'll shift her when I need to. She looks comfortable. So do you."

Joel grinned. "Waking to a kiss by my sexy-as-hell boyfriend? Why wouldn't I be comfortable?"

Marcus stroked Joel's cock under the blankets. He felt hard, and he wasn't the only one.

"I seem to need a little attention," Joel said. "What do you say to sharing a shower before breakfast?"

"Do we have time?" Marcus hated sounding so practical, but he didn't want Joel to get any flack at work for being late, especially as the gossip had probably already spread like wildfire.

"Quicker with two, and I figure it's responsible to save water." Joel pushed back the bedclothes onto the cat, who hissed her disapproval. He gave Marcus a very nice view of his backside and then disappeared in the direction of the bathroom.

Marcus didn't need a second invitation. Joel wet and soapy and...

"Sorry, cat," he mumbled, not feeling sorry in the least as he buried her in more bedclothes. She poked her head out and gave him a typical cat expression of disdain. "You'll have to deal."

~

"It feels kind of surreal having breakfast together." Joel had always enjoyed starting the day with someone rather than waking up alone.

"In a good way, I hope?" Marcus topped up his coffee and sat next to Joel. He'd already had one cup and was starting on his second, polishing off several Weet-Bix and a couple of pieces of toast and Vegemite in between cups.

"Yeah." Joel glanced at his cup of tea and bowl of cereal. "Where do you put all that food?"

Marcus laughed. The sound made Joel feel warm inside. Although Marcus claimed he didn't have much of a singing voice, his laugh had a musical quality to it.

"I often don't get lunch till late, depending on my schedule, so I always start my day with a good breakfast."

"I don't think I could eat that much for breakfast." Joel had never been a morning person, although he was better about it than he'd been. His job had forced him into it, and now he tended to burn the candle at both ends in an attempt to keep up with the increasing piles of paperwork.

"You made up for it over dinner last night."

"I'd worked up an appetite." Joel poked out his tongue at Marcus. "Besides, you ate more than I did."

"I told you I was hungry." Marcus's eyes twinkled. "And I never turn down good food. You're a good cook. That omelette was wonderful. I may have to keep you."

"You're keeping me for my cooking skills?" Joel put on a hangdog expression but only managed to keep it for a few moments before dissolving into laughter when Marcus rolled his eyes.

"Amongst other things." Marcus yawned and stretched, his T-shirt riding up to expose tanned skin over a flat stomach. "You do have several talents I'd like to explore further."

"Hmm, so do—" Joel's phone rang, interrupting their conversation. He strode over to the door and picked up his bag. "Damn it! Sorry, I should take this in case it's important." No one rang him this early in the morning.

"Take your time. I'm here if you need me."

Joel retrieved his phone from his bag and frowned when he read the name of the caller. "Hey, Bernie, what's up?"

"Hey, Joel, sorry to phone you this early, but I wanted to catch you before work. We've got a few minutes, right?"

"Yeah, I don't need to leave till seven thirty, so we're good." Joel tensed, wondering what shit was about to hit the fan. Bernadette sounded strained. She was worried about something, although she tried to hide it. "What's up?" he repeated.

Marcus put down his cup and walked over to Joel. "Okay?" he mouthed.

Joel shrugged.

"I just got a call from Mum," Bernadette said. "She rang an ambulance for Dad last night and—"

"Oh my God." Joel leaned heavily against the wall. Marcus slipped his arm around him and lowered them both to the floor. "Is he okay?"

"He's home now and resting. They spent most of the night at A&E, but the doctors sent him home about 5:00 a.m. with instructions to see his GP. Tests showed he'd had a minor heart attack, but he's insisting he's fine. He wouldn't let Mum phone me. She had to wait until he'd gone to bed."

"Your dad?" Marcus mouthed. "Okay?"

Joel nodded and then shrugged again. He felt tears welling but shoved his feeling of loss aside. His father had made his choice, yet... Damn it. Joel still loved his father and missed him like hell.

"It's okay," Marcus said softly. "I'm here," he repeated.

"I know," Joel whispered. "Does Mum know you've phoned me?" he asked Bernadette.

"Yes. She asked me to." Bernadette was quiet for a moment. "I thought the last one was supposed to be a warning. How many warnings does he need before it's too late?"

"I don't know. Dad's stubborn, and it takes a lot to make him take notice where his own health is concerned." Joel remembered the winter before he'd left. His father had kept working with a bad cough and refused to go to the doctor. By the time Jill had forced him to go, the cough had turned to pneumonia, and even then, it had taken some stern words by the doctor to get Claude to take time off work and rest.

"Yeah, that's what I'm worried about." Bernadette sighed. "But anyway, I thought you'd want to know, although there's not much we can do about it. He doesn't listen to me either."

"At least you still see him." Joel was surprised by the wistfulness in his voice. Damn it. He'd resigned himself to the fact years ago that he'd never talk to his father again.

"One of you has to make the move."

"It's not going to be me," Joel muttered.

"Stubborn, like Dad," Bernadette murmured.

"I heard that."

"You were meant to." Bernadette cleared her throat. "I didn't phone you to rehash all of that again. I... Anyway, now you know as much as I do."

"Yeah, thanks." Joel leaned into Marcus's embrace. "I really mean that. I do appreciate you calling."

"I know. I'm as stressed out by all this as you are. Mum wants to put off brunch this Saturday so she can keep an eye on Dad. Are you still okay for brunch as usual the fortnight after that? We could meet up before that without Mum if you want."

"Thanks, but I'll wait until we can all be there. That way we can talk to her together." Joel planned to talk to his mother before then about his father's health. Hopefully there would be a follow-up report from the doctor, but he wasn't counting on it.

"Is there someone you'd like to bring with you?"

"Excuse me?" How had Bernadette found out about Marcus? After all, Joel couldn't think of anyone else she would be talking about.

"I know you've got someone there with you. I heard him say something before." Bernadette sounded smug. "And given the time, he spent the night. Am I right?"

"Yeah, you're right. And that depends on whether he wants to come or not." Joel wasn't about to throw Marcus to the wolves without his permission first.

"Come or not to what?" Marcus asked. "I'm guessing the 'he' is me, and you haven't got some other guy I don't know about."

Joel chuckled. "Yeah. My sister wants to know if you want to join us for Saturday brunch in a couple of weeks. If you're working, that's fine. I'll tell her you're not free."

"Do you want me to tell her?" Marcus put his hand out for the phone, and Joel handed it over. "Hi, Bernadette. I'm Marcus." It didn't take a genius to figure out what Bernadette had said. "Yeah. I'm Joel's boyfriend. And yes, I'm Ella's brother. Looking forward to meeting you and your mum in a couple of weeks." Marcus winced. "No worries. Not going to happen even without your threat, but thanks all the same." He handed the phone back to Joel.

"He sounds hot," Bernadette said, "and I think he's a keeper."

"He is hot. What did you say to him? I hope you're playing nice."

"I always play nice." Bernadette practically purred into the phone. "See you both in a couple of Saturdays."

"See you." Joel tapped the phone's screen to end the call.

"Your sister is… interesting."

"What did she say to you?"

"She threatened to cut off my balls if I hurt you. I told her that wasn't going to happen." Marcus kissed Joel's cheek. "You okay? And is your dad going to be okay?"

Joel filled him in quickly with the part of the conversation he hadn't heard. "I guess time will tell," he said, untangling himself from Marcus's embrace, then standing. "Trouble is, the only warning Dad will heed is one that stops him dead in his tracks." He shivered at the choice of words—he hadn't thought, just spoken them.

"Hopefully your mum and sister can talk some sense into him." Marcus watched Joel shove his phone back into his bag. "Are you okay to go in to work? You could go in later and take some personal time this morning."

"I'll be fine." Joel would be better off with the distraction work would provide. "I have a staff meeting at eight and classes for the rest of the morning." He looked at his watch. "Shit. Sorry. I need to get going. Where do you need me to drop you off?"

"If you don't have time, I can catch a bus." Marcus shrugged. "Actually, why don't I do that, and then I can clean up the breakfast dishes before I leave. If that's okay with you."

Joel hesitated. As much as he wanted Marcus's company, he didn't trust himself to explain why he was late to work. If he started talking about his father, he was worried he wouldn't be able to stop. While his colleagues were support-ive, the less they knew about his relationship with his father, the better.

"I thought you had an early start," he said finally.

"I can be a bit later and work later at the end of the day to make up for it. It's not a problem." Marcus shrugged. "Besides, Brendan drives straight past here in about twenty minutes, and his first job is in Petone, so if the bus timetable doesn't cooperate, I'll get a ride from him to pick up my SUV."

"Okay, thanks." Joel kissed Marcus and grabbed his bag and keys. "Pull the front door shut on your way out. It should lock behind you." He paused at the kitchen doorway. "Do you want to come for dinner tonight, and maybe stay over again?"

Marcus smiled. "Yes! Definitely yes. I'll text you when I'm on my way, if that's okay. Although if you aim for dinner at seven, that should work."

"Great. Sounds like another date." Joel turned, walked back to Marcus, and kissed him again, this time long and hard. "Thank you," he whispered.

"Anytime. I'll stay as long as you want me to."

CHAPTER NINE

Marcus turned off the mower, removed his gloves, and reached for his vibrating phone. As front lawns went, this one was huge. Thankfully the back section was half the size, so wouldn't take him as long.

He read the caller ID and snorted. "Give it a rest, Garth," he muttered. As he shoved the phone into his pocket, it rang again. He swiped the screen, ready to give Garth a piece of his mind.

"Is this Marcus?"

He recognised her voice immediately. "Hi, Bernadette. What can I do for you?"

"I hope you don't mind me calling you. I got your number from one of your business cards. Ella gave one to me the last time we met for lunch."

"Ah, okay." Marcus hadn't known his sister and Joel's were meeting for lunch. He filed the information away to tell Joel that evening.

"Have I got you at a bad time?"

"No, it's fine. I was about to take a break anyway. It's hot out today." Marcus grabbed his water bottle while he waited for her to continue. He wasn't used to the last week of March being so humid, and despite a few rainy days when the temperature had dropped, autumn looked like it would be much later than usual.

"This morning was a little awkward and not quite the introduction I'd planned." Bernadette paused as though unsure how to continue.

"You did the right thing calling Joel. He needs to know what's going on with your dad."

"How's he doing? Really?"

"Apart from working through what you told him this morning, he's great." Marcus smiled despite knowing she couldn't see him. "He's a good guy, and I plan to take good care of him." That was about as much as he was prepared to tell her. "I think this is probably a conversation you should be having with him, don't you?"

"I've tried, and although he talks about almost everything, this is one subject he shuts down about. I could tell this morning that you care for him, and I..." Bernadette let out a huge sigh. "Sorry, he's my baby brother, and it's good to know there's someone looking out for him."

"Darin and Ella have always been there for him."

"I know I haven't always. It was Ella's idea to start these regular brunch get-togethers. She talked Joel into coming that first time."

"Ah." That made a lot of sense. "Ella's not easy to argue with once she's set her mind to something."

For someone who had only just met him, and then briefly over the phone, Bernadette was getting into some very personal stuff. She reminded him of Joel in that.

"No, she isn't. Sorry to have bothered you. If you want to tell Joel I called, that's okay. Sisters are allowed to be concerned, right?"

"Right." Marcus knew better than to sound like he was

dismissing Bernadette's concerns. She was obviously worried about her brother and making an effort to improve things between them. "I will, and no problem. Break's over, and I need to get back to work. Looking forward to meeting you properly in a couple of weeks."

"Yeah, me too. Bye." She hung up before Marcus had the chance to reply.

He took another swig of water and then got back to finishing the job. He'd barely completed the last stretch of lawn when his phone vibrated again. "Bernadette?" Although she'd finished their call, he had a nagging feeling she hadn't said everything she'd wanted to.

"Hi, Marcus." Marcus felt a familiar knot in the base of his stomach. He checked his caller ID—something he should have done instead of presuming he knew who it was.

"Garth," Marcus said cautiously. Perhaps he had treated Garth unfairly by ignoring all his texts and calls. A more reasonable polite approach might work better. "Umm, how are you?"

"Fine. Good to know you're settling in up there—and got yourself a girlfriend."

"Excuse me?"

"Bernadette? I didn't realise you're bi like me."

"I'm not. She's my boyfriend's sister."

"Ah, okay." Garth hesitated before continuing. "It's strange not seeing you around. I had hoped we'd keep in touch. I know we fought a bit those last few months, but I still consider you my friend. Too much water under the bridge not to."

"I've already told you how I feel about that. I'm sorry, but—"

"I'm sorry too, for everything that happened."

It took Marcus a couple of seconds to figure out Garth's voice was no longer coming from his phone. *Bloody hell.* He'd been so focused on the call, he hadn't noticed Garth approaching.

"What are you doing here?" Marcus wasn't sure whether to feel shocked or angry. He'd told Garth he'd be working with Brendan, so he guessed it hadn't taken much detective work on Garth's part to find him. Garth had always managed to work out where Marcus was at any given time when they had been living together. That much hadn't changed at least.

Garth smiled, and he chuckled as though amused by Marcus's reaction. "Is that all I get after all these months? I've missed you, and I figured if we're going to have this conversation, the least I could do is make the effort to have it in person."

"Are you up here on business?"

"I'm here to see you."

"Oh." Marcus felt a sudden pang of guilt. In not answering Garth's calls, he hadn't left Garth much choice. "Sorry," he mumbled.

Garth closed the distance between them and pulled Marcus into a firm embrace, his touch lingering longer for someone who was now just a friend. Marcus could smell Garth's aftershave, the scent reminding him of how much he used to enjoy being in Garth's arms like this.

"So am I." Garth let go of Marcus and took a moment to study him. "You're looking well. You always did look good when you were working." He cleared his throat. "Thing is, I have something I need to tell you, and as you kept ignoring my attempts to contact you..."

"I told you we're over. We had this conversation before I left Hokitika." The years they'd spent together were quickly feeling like a lifetime ago. More so since he'd started dating Joel. "And it isn't a talk we should have while I'm working."

If Garth didn't make his point and quickly, Marcus would have to tell him to leave.

"I've found someone else, and I wanted you to find out from me."

"I appreciate that."

Garth hadn't cheated on him—he knew that for certain. Although they'd drifted apart, Garth lived by high moral standards, and he'd never lied.

"You remember Felicity Munroe?" Garth indicated the bench seat by the side fence and gestured for Marcus to join him.

"Yeah. Her family lives in Greymouth?"

Marcus and Garth had met her at an A&P—Agricultural and Pastoral—show in Wanaka the year before. Marcus hesitated and then sat next to Garth. If Garth was so determined to talk to him that he'd travelled to Wellington to do so, the least Marcus could do was be civil.

"Yes, that's her. She moved to Hokitika and is managing one of the local cafés. We met up again shortly after you left for Wellington." Garth's tone grew warmer. He obviously had feelings for her. "You said you have a boyfriend?"

"Yes," Marcus confirmed. Garth tilted his head to the side and pushed his glasses up his nose, his usual gesture when he was waiting for more information. "His name is Joel, and we're very happy together."

Garth was his past. Joel was his future. He wasn't ready for the two to collide in an already awkward meeting. Although Joel was at school, Marcus couldn't help glancing around to make sure he and Garth didn't have an audience. Not only that, but he usually tried to avoid personal stuff while he was working.

"That's nice." Garth cleared his throat again. "Thing is. I miss you, and I don't want to make a mistake by moving forward if there's a chance we could get back together. It's not fair to Felicity, and it's not fair on us either."

"There is no us." So the warmth Marcus had heard in Garth's voice wasn't because of Felicity.

"There used to be." Garth lowered his voice into the husky whisper Marcus once loved so much and put his hand on Marcus's knee.

Marcus's heart sped up. Garth had always known where to touch him and how, and exactly how long to wait so Marcus would beg for more. And now... Marcus remembered how it felt to have that hand on his stomach, Garth's warm, moist touch sliding lower—

Marcus swallowed. He took a swig of water, trying to ignore his body's reaction to a relationship that was long over. "There's still no us." Marcus's voice trembled despite his determination to be firm. "You need to leave. I'm working, and you shouldn't be here."

"Oh, come on. You want me. I can hear it in your voice, and I can see the way you're trembling. All couples fall out from time to time. Why don't you come home, and we can give it another go?"

"I am home." Marcus removed Garth's hand from his knee and took another swig of water. Sweat trickled down the back of his neck. "We're over. I left Hokitika to start a new life. You should do the same. You don't need my permission."

"You always were cold." Garth took off his glasses and polished them on the bottom of his shirt, like he always did when he didn't like something Marcus said. "I hope this new guy of yours knows what he's getting into."

"That's none of your business." Marcus's mouth felt suddenly dry, despite the water he'd been drinking.

"Still not talking about stuff, I see. At least I'm trying to change. Well, don't come crying to me when you and this Joel have the same issues we did."

What issues? Marcus had left because they'd drifted apart,

and Garth had expected them to spend all their free time together. The little personal space they'd had when they'd first got together had shrunk with each passing year.

"I wasn't planning to." Despite everything Garth had said, Marcus didn't want their last conversation to be an argument. Better if he took a few extra minutes and finished things for good. The last thing he needed was to give Garth the impression they should talk again later. "Look, I'm sorry things didn't last between us. But it is over. You should go out with Felicity. At least give the relationship a chance."

"I'm planning to." Garth twisted Marcus's words to suit his own situation.

Marcus had forgotten how good Garth was at doing that. Seeing him had made all the bad stuff that had niggled him for years disappear until Garth reminded him all too well why they'd broken up. Marcus had distanced himself emotionally from Garth bit by bit as the cracks in their relationship had become harder to ignore.

An awkward silence stretched between them.

"I'm sorry," Garth whispered. He started for reach for Marcus's hand and then stopped. "I've stepped over a line. I wanted to talk to you, and it hurts knowing you've found someone else already. I meant what I said about missing you. I'd still like to be friends."

"Yeah, you have, and I thought we still were." Marcus knew he'd screwed up by ignoring Garth's efforts to stay in touch, but he hadn't known how else to handle the situation. "I told you I needed some distance between us first."

"I don't regret those years we were together, you know?" Garth sounded apologetic, but then he'd always been good at backtracking after he'd shoved his foot in his mouth. "I'm sorry things didn't work out, but… I needed to make sure."

"I hope it works out for you with Felicity, but I think you should go. There's nothing here for you. We're done." Marcus's tone sounded cooler than he intended. He winced, hearing Garth's accusation repeating in his mind.

"You'll at least keep in touch?" Garth stood. "I'll give it a few months before I try to contact you again. Promise."

"Thanks." Marcus deliberately kept sitting. He felt cold inside. "Take care, Garth."

"You too, and good luck to you and Joel. You're going to need it." Garth hesitated as though he was waiting for Marcus to react, but when nothing happened, he turned and walked down the driveway.

Marcus let out a long breath. One conversation, and everything they'd had together came flooding back. If he'd had any doubts—which he hadn't—that he and Garth were over, he didn't now. He hadn't lied about hoping Garth's new relationship worked out, but he didn't want to hear from him again.

Especially if Garth tried to rekindle a flame that hadn't been burning brightly for a longer time than Marcus wanted to admit.

Then why had it only taken a few words and a simple touch to remind Marcus of what they'd had?

Marcus obviously hadn't moved on as much as he'd thought he had. A little voice in his head suggested that he should probably talk to Joel about it, but he wasn't sure that was a great idea. Maybe he could ignore it, the same way he'd ignored Garth's attempts to contact him.

Yeah, because that would work. He'd promised Joel he'd talk about things. He'd never had that with Garth, and life had been a lot simpler because of it, but simpler wasn't always better.

What he'd had with Garth was nothing compared to what he was sure he could have with Joel, and he wanted this new relationship to work. Starting out by keeping things to himself—something he'd accused Garth of—wasn't the way to go.

~

The knock at the door had to be Marcus. Joel filled a glass of water with shaking hands and took a long drink, giving himself a few moments to regain his composure. Why the hell hadn't he cancelled dinner tonight? He'd thought he could do this, but now he wasn't so sure.

Marcus knocked again.

Joel took a deep breath, and flung a tea-towel over his shoulder, focusing on the weight of it instead of the visuals replaying in his mind. "Hey." He kept his tone light when he opened the front door. Marcus deserved the chance to explain himself.

Didn't he?

He forced himself not to pull away when Marcus greeted him with a kiss on the cheek.

"Everything okay?" Marcus deposited his backpack by the door. Was he still planning to stay over?

"You tell me." Joel turned and walked back into the kitchen. "I got some fish, as we… I thought as you hadn't the chance to catch it yourself for a while, you might like some." He'd already picked it up on his way home at lunchtime that day so figured they might as well have it.

"Thanks, sounds great." Marcus frowned. He turned Joel to face him. "What's wrong? And don't tell me it's nothing. I can hear it in your voice." His tone softened. "Did something else happen with your dad."

"He had his hand on your knee!" Joel blurted out.

Marcus cringed. "Excuse me?"

"Garth had his fucking hand on your knee." Joel met Marcus's gaze. He looked all kinds of guilty. "I was driving past at lunchtime and saw you and Garth in a bloody embrace. You told me you guys were over."

"You saw us?" *Us*, not *me*. At least Marcus wasn't trying to deny it. "And we are. Garth and me I meant. Not us." Marcus's voice shook. "I hope. Oh hell. Look, I know what it must have looked like…"

"Oh really?" Joel backed up towards the table. "It looked like you guys were being very friendly, like you hadn't broken up at all." His voice cracked, despite his determination to keep his composure. "I'm not going to be your thing on the side. I can't be with someone who isn't honest with me. I'm not going through that again." He poked Marcus in the chest. "I can't be with someone who does a whole lot of shit they don't tell me about until I *need* to know about it."

"I was going to tell you tonight, honest." Marcus sat down on one of the kitchen chairs and buried his face in his hands. "Bloody Garth. He wouldn't take no for an answer, so he turned up today. I had no idea he was in Wellington, I swear."

"But?"

"He wanted to make sure we were done." Marcus's voice dropped to a whisper. "And to ask if we might get back together again."

"What did you tell him?" Joel's heart raced. Oh God. He'd been such an idiot, falling for Marcus. He'd been so convinced Marcus wanted a future together. Last night had been wonderful, and it had felt so right.

Marcus looked up. "I told him I had a boyfriend, and it sure as hell wasn't him. Garth and I are done. I wouldn't do that to you." Hurt chased surprise across his face. "Do you really think I'd cheat on you? Fuck. No."

"I want to believe you, but… I came home to pick up some paperwork, slowed down when I saw your SUV, hoping to see you. I wasn't expecting that." Joel couldn't forget what he'd seen.

"He told me I hadn't changed, then he wished me luck with you, and said I'd need it." Marcus's tone flattened. He studied the floor. "He hugged me, and then I couldn't... I'm sorry. Yeah, he did what you saw, and I should have put a stop to the conversation a lot sooner than I did. I was with the guy for years. My heart and mind don't want him, but I guess my body is still playing catch up." He sounded miserable.

Joel edged closer. "So what I saw was only part of it," he said slowly, "and you still want me?"

Marcus frowned. "Of course I still want you! I meant everything I said and did last night. If I'd known you'd seen us I would have come around sooner, but I had no clue." He stood. "If you want me to leave, I will."

"Do you want to?" Joel felt like a total heel. He'd seen a snatch of something bigger and immediately thought the worst. "Garth's been an arsehole, but I haven't been much better. I'm sorry too."

"I'm not sure how I would have reacted if I'd seen you and Reed together." Marcus stayed standing yet didn't attempt to move closer. "What we have is very new. I wonder why you'd even want to be with someone like me. Garth... I left him, and it's true we'd drifted apart, but I pushed him away too, when thing started to go wrong." Marcus shrugged. "He's not totally wrong about me being cold."

"Bastard." Joel refocused his anger onto the man who deserved it.

Marcus flinched.

"I meant Garth, not you," Joel added quickly.

"I want to be good for you." Marcus looked down when Nannerl sat on his feet, gazed up at him, and meowed. "I want to be able to talk to you about everything, but if you hadn't brought it up now, I'm scared I would have bottled up the whole thing for weeks." He bent to pat the cat. His hand shook.

Joel walked over to Marcus and pulled him into a hug. "You wonder why *I* want to be with *you*?" Joel shook his head in disbelief. "No, I'm the one who should wonder. Why would someone as hot as you—a guy who is intelligent, easygoing, and not to mention fantastic in bed—want someone like me? I talk too much, especially when I'm nervous, I work long hours, and you've already been introduced to my wonderfully dysfunctional relationship with my father."

"Because I… you're the guy I want." Marcus seemed surprised at Joel's confession. "You're totally the best thing in my life." He squeezed Joel's hand.

Joel kissed him softly. "Why don't we move into the living room and talk?" he suggested. Dinner could keep. Now that they were talking, Joel didn't want to risk stopping again until they'd both said everything they needed to say.

"Okay." Marcus followed Joel out to the living room, still holding Joel's hand.

Once they were seated, Joel cleared his throat. "I… I don't deal well with people not telling me things." He continued quickly when Marcus began to look guilty again. "You're not the only one still dealing with shit from your last boyfriend. One of the last arguments I had with Reed was about him not telling me about something I needed to know."

"Sometimes I need a bit of prompting but I want to keep trying. I want to be the person you need. I'm not Reed, and I don't want to be." Marcus chewed on his lower lip.

"We're talking about something that happened earlier today, so I think we're fine." Joel leaned his forehead against Marcus's. "I'm sorry. I guess we're still working on learning to trust each other, yeah?"

Marcus brushed back a strand of Joel's hair when it flopped over one eye before leaning back against the sofa. "I thought you broke up with Reed because he asked you to move to Australia with him and you didn't want to go."

"Yeah, well. What kind of guy asks that after he's already taken the job over there and booked two one-way tickets? He was so certain I'd go along with what he wanted because I always had, that he didn't bother to ask me what *I* wanted." Joel hadn't told anyone that before, not even Darin. In fact, he'd tried to forget it himself and focus on the story he wanted to believe—the version of the truth he'd told everyone, including Marcus.

"Ouch." Marcus turned so they were facing each other again. "I would never do something without asking you first. I don't presume, okay? And I promise I'll never take you for granted."

"Okay. Sorry." Joel hadn't realised why he'd overreacted until he'd finally told the truth out loud. "I guess that last situation with Reed affected me more than I thought it had. I convinced myself I was okay, and then when you... I saw the same thing start to happen all over again. Which is crazy, considering Reed and I were together for years, and you and I are very new at this."

"I'm not Reed," Marcus repeated softly, "although since I didn't handle that conversation with Garth very well this afternoon, I'm probably just as much of an idiot right now."

"You're not an idiot," Joel said. "I think that's me."

"We've both got baggage. No one gets to our age without it. We're not twentysomethings in our first relationship. I had a couple of boyfriends before Garth."

"Yeah," Joel said. "It wasn't as though Reed was the guy I came out to my dad for. That guy broke up with me a couple of weeks later."

"His loss." Marcus grew quiet for a moment, and when he spoke again, his words were measured, as though he'd given them a lot of thought. "What we have is very different from my relationship with Garth. I moved up here to get away from him because I couldn't go anywhere in Hokitika without hearing about him and how wonderful he is." He shrugged. "He is a good guy, most of the time, and we *were* happy for a good few years before I figured out he wasn't *my* guy."

"We've both got some crap we're carrying around." At least Marcus had the excuse that his breakup wasn't that long ago. Joel had wanted to think he'd put Reed well behind him. If five years wasn't enough, how long would it take?

"I can hear you thinking from here." Marcus kissed Joel's forehead. "I'm sorry. You cooked a lovely meal, and this should have been a nice evening."

"It still can be. We've talked about what happened, so let's both move on, hmm?"

"I definitely want to keep you." Marcus kissed Joel again, this time on the lips—slow, deep, and full of promise and desire.

"Ditto." How could Joel have thought Marcus was having second thoughts and wanting to be with someone else? Marcus's expression made Joel's breath hitch, and it showed how much he wanted their relationship to work. "Dinner will keep a bit longer. I want to show you how much I want you first. Really want you."

Marcus smiled. "As long as I get to show you second. Or better yet, let's do it together."

CHAPTER TEN

Joel read the text, chuckled, and put his phone back in his pocket. "That was Bernie. They're running late but should be here soon." He took a sip of his coffee. "They're always late for some reason or another, although it's usually because of Mum. According to Bernie, anyway."

"I don't mind waiting a while. It gives us some extra time before they get here." Marcus returned the waitress's smile—Joel had introduced her as Wendy—and admired the decor. "I haven't been here before. It's nice."

"Yeah. Good service and food at a reasonable price. We thought about trying different cafés, but then figured as we'd found one we really liked, why not stick to it?"

"I thought you liked change?"

"I do, but Mum doesn't. She's very much a creature of habit. When I was growing up, I always knew what I'd be getting for dinner depending on what day of the week it was."

"Nothing wrong with that." Marcus studied the mural on the wall. "I can see why the decor would appeal. It's relaxing. The artist has done a great job in capturing the feel of the harbour, and the musical theme reminds me of you." He reached for Joel's hand and squeezed it, offering a smile he hoped was reassuring.

Joel nodded and squeezed back. "That obvious I'm nervous, huh?"

"Yeah, a bit. So am I."

This meeting was important to both of them. Marcus had spoken to Joel's sister over the phone a few times since her phone call a month ago, but it wasn't the same as meeting her in person. Although Joel had said his mother had finally accepted that Reed had been more than a close friend, he had no clue how she'd react to meeting Marcus. Knowing her son was gay was a very different thing to being confronted by the proof of it.

"I'm still trying to figure out where the holidays went." Joel changed the subject. "Seems like only yesterday it was Easter and I had two weeks of no school to look forward to." He sighed. "Back to work on Monday, and there's only six weeks until the concert."

"You're not regretting saying yes to doing it, are you?" Marcus had been concerned about how hard Joel worked through the holidays. While he knew teachers didn't get much of a break between terms, Joel had taken the Easter weekend off and then dived straight back into work. Marcus had gone around to Joel's a few times and cooked for him to make sure he ate properly.

"The concert's fine and under control." Joel waved his hand, gesturing to Marcus not to worry about it. "I'm planning to sit down and get a decent practise session of my own in this afternoon." He grimaced. "That piece never gave me problems before but there are a couple of bars I keep stuffing up. I used to enjoy performing, but perhaps it's been too long. Conducting is different."

"I think it sounds great." The glimpses Marcus saw of Joel

as a musician never failed to blow him away. "I'm sure it will on the night of the concert too."

"Yeah, well." Joel shrugged. "There's always room for improvement, right? However I feel about it, I can't back down now and still expect the kids to perform. It reeks of double standards."

"As long as you don't push yourself too hard and you take care of yourself. I've heard you tell your students that mistakes happen and not to beat themselves up over them. If you make a mistake, I doubt anyone but you will know." Marcus paused. "Do you mind if I mow your lawns and do a bit of weeding this afternoon? I can come another day if the noise will be too distracting."

"Sounds good, and thank you." Joel leaned in and whispered, "You know it won't be the noise that distracts me, right?"

"Umm." Marcus thought he'd better come clean. "That was sort of the plan, yeah, and you'll need a break, right? I don't mind providing one."

Joel grinned. "Good, because I'm going to hold you to that." He kissed Marcus on the cheek. Although the kiss was chaste, the way Joel ran his hand up Marcus's leg under the table definitely wasn't. "Later," he murmured, his breath hot against Marcus's cheek.

"Hell, yes." Marcus's heart sped up. He took a few deep breaths as a reminder they were in a public place.

Joel kissed Marcus again, this time on the lips in a way that promised much more, but he broke the kiss quickly when someone called his name from the café door.

"Joel!"

Marcus recognised Bernadette's voice immediately. He wouldn't have picked her as Joel's sister from a distance. While Joel was tall, Bernadette was petite, her blonde hair contrasting with his much darker shade. An older woman followed her, glancing around the café until her gaze settled on Joel, and she smiled.

"Over here!" Joel waved to them.

As they came closer, Marcus could see the resemblance more easily. Bernadette had the same twinkle in her eyes that he'd seen in Joel's. Joel must have taken after his father in looks, while Bernadette resembled her mother, except for her eyes, which were a darker blue.

Joel stood as his mother approached, and Marcus followed his lead.

"Mum," Joel said, "this is Marcus. Marcus, this is my mum, Jill. You've spoken to my sister before." He gave Bernadette a pointed look. "A couple of times, actually."

"Nice to meet you, Mrs Ashcroft." Marcus shook her hand. "And to finally meet you in person, Bernadette."

"You too, Marcus." Jill sat, and then her children did too. "And please call me Jill. Mrs Ashcroft is far too formal, don't you think?"

"Okay... Jill." Marcus smiled. He liked her already and appreciated her attempt to put him at ease.

"Nice to finally meet you properly," Bernadette said. "I'm surprised you guys are sitting inside. There are plenty of tables free outside. Are you changing your habits? You grabbed an inside table last time too."

"I wanted to show Marcus the mural, and we kind of settled here," Joel said. "Do you want to shift outside? It's no problem if you do."

"I think this table is just fine." Jill caught the eye of the waitress. "Wendy, we'd like to order now, please. I'll have the usual. Bernadette?"

"The usual, and we'll share a pot of tea, thanks."

Joel studied the menu. "A ham and mushroom omelette for me today."

"I'll have a ham and cheese toasted sandwich, please." Marcus turned to Joel. "Do you want a refill on your coffee?"

"Sounds good." Joel returned his menu to Wendy.

"Thanks. Won't be long." Wendy smiled. "Enjoy your conversation."

"So... you're not planning to skip lunch today, Joel?" Bernadette said. "I told you Marcus was good for him," she told her mother.

"I have lunch most days," Joel said. "This is brunch, in case you've forgotten. That meal that combines both breakfast and lunch."

"Ah, yes, I've vaguely heard of that." Bernadette grinned and looked smug.

Jill sighed. "Don't mind them," she told Marcus. "Five minutes in the same room together and they can't resist teasing each other."

"It's fine," Marcus said. "I'm quite enjoying it, actually, and Joel does have a tendency to skip meals at times."

"Traitor," muttered Joel, although he had a twinkle in his eye. He slid his hand under the table and took hold of Marcus's hand.

"So, Bernadette tells me you're Ella's brother," Jill said. "Lovely girl. I can see the family resemblance."

"Yes, I am." Marcus hadn't expected her to start with the questions so soon, although Joel had warned him she probably would. "I moved up here from Hokitika in February. I'm staying with my sister and her family until I find a place of my own."

He was spending more time at Joel's than at Ella's at present, but he wasn't about to tell Joel's mother that.

"It's important to get used to a place first." Jill looked up and gave Wendy a nod when she delivered the tea. "Thank you. Bernadette, would you mind pouring? I always manage to dribble some of the tea onto the tablecloth. You have a much steadier hand than I do."

Bernadette poured the tea and handed Jill a cup. "Do you think you'll stay in Wellington, Marcus?"

"I'm planning to." Marcus took a sip of his coffee. "There's a lot to keep me here, and business is growing, so having enough work isn't going to be an issue either."

"You mow lawns for a living?" Jill phrased it as a question, although Joel had already told her.

"Yes, that's right, and some gardening." He felt Joel caress his hand with his thumb and smiled. "I'm hoping to expand it to include a few other things. With so many people working long hours now, there's more of a demand for someone who can do the odd jobs they don't have time to do themselves."

"Yes, I imagine there would be." Jill sounded thoughtful. "You've never thought about doing anything else?"

"No. I enjoy what I do. It's very satisfying seeing a job well done."

Jill smiled. "I've heard my husband Claude say the same thing when he's finished a project. He built his business up from nothing, you know. He's always worked hard. I hear the same pride in your voice as I hear in his. It's important to love what you do. I know a lot of people don't, but it's good if you can." She turned to Bernadette. "Don't you think so?"

"Yes, Mum," Bernadette mumbled.

Marcus raised an eyebrow, but Joel shook his head with a warning not to pursue that comment further.

"How is Dad?" Joel asked. "Is he still doing okay?"

"Oh yes." Jill took another sip of tea and waited for Wendy to set their meals on the table. After the waitress had left, she continued slowly. "The doctors say he could be fine for a long time, but if it happens again, they'll have to consider an operation to put a stent in. It's fairly straightfor-ward from what I gather, but your father isn't—"

"He's ignoring the situation and hoping it will go away so he doesn't have to deal with it," Bernadette added.

"Nothing new there." Joel gripped Marcus's hand tightly.

"He used to listen to you, Joel," Jill said. "I did hope you two might put your differences behind you and work things out. It would mean a great deal to him. He does miss you."

Joel tensed. "Sure he does. Dad hasn't listened to my opinion in nearly twenty years. Not since I told him I was gay, and that isn't going to change." He placed his and Marcus's joined hands on the table and edged closer to Marcus. "You really think he'd listen to me when he's not okay with me having a boyfriend?"

"Your father is a stubborn man." Jill sighed. "You both are. That is what worries me. I do wish you'd talk to each other again. This has gone on long enough."

Marcus glanced between Jill and Joel. He casually put an arm around Joel, showing his support for him, without butting into a very personal conversation.

"I don't think this is the place to bring all that up, do you?" Bernadette whispered. "And in front of Joel's boyfriend?"

"Marcus already knows all about it, and anything you say to me, you can say in front of him," Joel said evenly. "But yeah. Why bring this up now, when you've spent years avoiding it?"

Jill put down her fork and wiped the side of her mouth with her napkin although she hadn't begun her meal. "Seeing Claude ill and in hospital last month wasn't… pleasant. If something happened, he could die without ever mending his relationship with you. I love both of you, and I don't want that to happen." She gave Marcus a nod. "I'm sorry to bring this up here, but I saw the two of you together, and it's very obvious you care for each other. I'm not sure there ever will be a right time to talk about this, so

I thought I'd take the bull by the horns and dive straight in."

"You never said anything when I left. You never spoke to me for years."

"I was wrong. I'm sorry." Jill cleared her throat. "I didn't want to take sides, but I guess I did anyway. I never thought it would go as far or as long as it has." Jill picked up her fork and started eating her omelette, clearly embarrassed by the whole conversation.

Joel had told Marcus that his mother rarely stated her opinions on anything but instead went along with everything his father did. She must have done a lot of soul-searching before bringing up the sensitive subject of Joel and Claude's relationship. Marcus admired her for that.

Unfortunately he had no clue how to fix the awkward silence that now hung across the table like a heavy fog. He glanced at Bernadette, hoping she'd have the answer he lacked.

Bernadette cleared her throat. "How are the rehearsals for your concert coming along?"

Joel took a long swig of coffee. When he spoke again, he sounded more like himself. "Still some work to do, but the kids are doing great."

"Are you coming to the concert, Marcus?" Bernadette asked.

"I wouldn't miss it for the world."

"We'll look forward to seeing you there." Jill topped up her tea, ignoring the dribbles of brown liquid that showered the table. "Have you heard Joel play piano? He used to be very good. I loved listening to him practise."

"He's still very good," Marcus told her. "I've sat in on a couple of rehearsals, and I think he's doing an amazing job with the kids. He's a very gifted teacher."

Joel flushed. "I think you might be a little biased."

"I'm allowed to be, but that doesn't mean what I say isn't the truth." Marcus let go of Joel but kept close, their legs brushing together under the table. He picked up his sandwich and started to eat. "The food here is very good."

"The service is good too." Jill watched Joel and Marcus together and gave Marcus a smile. The way her eyes twinkled reminded him of Joel. "I'm glad Joel's found you, and I hope we'll see more of you at these brunches." She turned to Bernadette. "Perhaps you could ask a friend to watch the boys so Keith could join us sometime. I'm sure he'd like to meet Marcus too."

"Thanks. I'd like that." Marcus took another swig of coffee. "The brunches *and* meeting Keith, I mean."

"Are you enjoying your stay in Wellington?" Jill stirred her tea although she hadn't added any sugar. "I hope Joel has shown you some of the sights."

"Marcus is living here now," Joel reminded her. "There's plenty of time for that."

"It's never too soon and you can't work all the time." Jill gave him the patented Mum look. While not exactly disapproval, it reeked of thoughtful concern with a healthy helping of *how many times have I told you that?*

"You should take the cable car up to Kelburn if you haven't already," Bernadette added. "Keith and I used to do that before we were married. We'd walk down through the botanical gardens. The rose gardens are very pretty."

"I'm really busy at the moment," Joel murmured.

"Sounds lovely," Marcus said at the same time.

Joel ducked his head. "I… Are you guys trying to hint that I'm working too hard? If you are, it's not very subtle."

"You? Work too hard?" Bernadette snorted. "Whatever would have given us that idea?" She chuckled at Joel's incredulous look. "Of course we're hinting you should take a break. You're like Dad in that. Even after the doctor told him to slow down, he only stays in and does office work a few days a week. I'm sure being out on-site the rest of the week isn't good for him. Marcus, you must have noticed how hard Joel works. Right?"

Marcus glanced at Jill, hoping she'd come to his rescue, but she'd picked up her handbag and was looking inside for something. "Umm... maybe?"

Joel dug him in the ribs. "You're supposed to be on my side!"

"I am." Marcus took a breath and blew it out. "But your sister has a point. You do work too hard. I'm allowed to be concerned."

"Fine." Joel held up his hands in surrender. "I promise to be a good boy and take an afternoon off here and there, okay?"

Bernadette raised an eyebrow. "At last! Someone he'll actually listen to."

"I speak up if something needs saying—but he's free to make up his own mind." Marcus glanced at Joel. "He knows that. And he does the same for me."

"Fair enough, I guess." Bernadette glanced between them.

Jill took a small card from her handbag and slipped it under Marcus's plate. "In case you need to contact me."

"Bernadette already has his number," Joel said.

"Ella gave me his business card." Bernadette shrugged. She poked out her tongue at her brother.

"Whatever," Joel retorted.

Jill chuckled. "Welcome to our family, Marcus. It's lovely to have you here."

CHAPTER ELEVEN

"Do you mind driving?" Joel asked Marcus when they reached the car. Jill had talked to him for a few minutes while Marcus and Bernadette had gone up to the counter to settle the bill.

"Sure, no problem." Marcus took the keys and slid into the driver's seat. "Everything okay? Did your mum say something to you?"

"Yeah. I'm a bit distracted, I guess." Joel fastened his seat belt and reached for Marcus's hand, then held it for a moment before letting go when Marcus started the engine. "You know how to get onto the motorway from here, right?"

"Yeah, I'll be fine. I've been into town a few times with Darin, so I know my way around." Marcus didn't ask any more questions, although he gave Joel a kiss on the cheek before he pulled out into traffic.

Joel snuggled into his seat, half closing his eyes, half taking in the scenery as Marcus headed for the motorway. It was busy for a Saturday afternoon, and it took a while for them to reach Waterloo Quay. Children played at Frank Kitts

Park on their right, and one of the Picton ferries slowly made its way across the harbour.

Joel hated it when his mother was right. Although he was relieved she'd finally decided to have an opinion about his relationship with his father, now that she had, he wished she'd leave the subject alone. She'd tried to get Claude to contact Joel, but he was as stubborn as ever.

Damn it. Joel had thought they'd left that can of worms behind in the restaurant when the conversation had changed tack.

Joel's father aside, Marcus fitted into their family dynamics well, and both Jill and Bernadette liked him. Joel had worried for a moment that Bernadette had convinced Marcus to join her on the dark side in her quest to get Joel to work less.

Honestly. He shook his head. Why couldn't his sister see how much work he had to do? Schoolwork didn't plan or mark itself, and he was determined to make this concert a success. Once he got past June, he could relax a bit. A few more weeks at his current pace, and his hard work would pay off.

"You want to go straight home?"

Marcus's question made Joel look up in surprise. "Huh?"

"I need to know what lane to get into," Marcus explained.

"Home." Joel added, "Please."

Marcus glanced at him. "Are you sure? You look like you could use some time out."

"Yeah." Joel straightened up. Marcus probably had a point. Despite having slept in a bit later that morning, Joel still felt tired. He jabbed at the button to lower the car window and breathed in the fresh air. The temperature had dropped, and grey clouds chased one another across the otherwise blue sky.

Marcus didn't push Joel to elaborate. At least not out

loud. Joel had discovered that one of the reasons Marcus didn't need to always say much was that his silence spoke volumes.

"I can hear your thoughts from here," Joel said.

"Good." Marcus glanced at Joel again. "I'm concerned. Something's up. You're too quiet."

"Sorry. I... I'm... I'm not doing so well." Joel kept his tone light. If he talked about how he felt, he'd never stop. "Guess you do that thing where you say stuff without saying it better than me, huh?"

"Just because I do that doesn't mean I should. If you feel you can talk, I'll listen.

Once they reached Petone, Marcus parked the car in front of the foreshore by the wharf. A couple of children collected driftwood on the beach, their father keeping a watchful eye on them and taking the occasional photo with his phone. Seagulls circled overhead, already heading inland in preparation for the coming rain.

"Okay, I get the message." Joel sighed. "But if we're going to talk, can I at least choose where?"

"Of course." Marcus didn't restart the engine. "I know I'm not great at talking about the things I should, so I probably have a nerve expecting you to, but... even if you don't want to, I... I just want to be here for you, okay?"

Joel smiled. "Thanks, and I appreciate it." He stared out at the ocean for a few minutes. "There's a place I like to go to think," he said finally. "I'd like to show it to you."

"Thanks. I'd like that." Marcus pulled Joel into a hug. "I do lo—care about you. I think whatever you need to talk about is something you've needed to get off your chest for a while."

"Yeah." Joel hung on to Marcus tightly, then forced himself to let go. Being in Marcus's arms made him feel safe, but he couldn't expect Marcus to charge in like some knight in shining armour and save the day. That kind of thing worked great in stories, but reality was way more complicated. "But not here. Head home, but don't turn off where you usually do. I'll show you where to go."

"Okay." Marcus pulled back out into traffic.

Joel wasn't sure how exactly he was going to put what he felt into words. He knew what he *wanted* to say, but he'd never talked to anyone about how he felt. Although he'd spoken of his relationship with his father in bits and pieces, he'd been careful to keep his emotions out of it, apart from that embarrassing dinner at Darin's nearly three months ago. However, his mother's words had struck a nerve.

"Straight through here and second on the left. We're going to follow the road for a minute or so and pull in before we reach the footbridge to Te Whiti Park. I'll tell you when."

The road was slow going with several speed humps, and a stream ran alongside it. Small families of ducks swam together, although one loner had gone ahead. In the distance Joel could hear shouting and cheering from the sports field at the park, but they weren't close enough to make out any words.

"Pull in here." Joel waited until Marcus had locked the car, then taking Marcus's hand in his, led him across the road to the stream.

Trees of all sizes lined the grassy bank, some high enough to climb, others only a few years old. Across from where they'd left the car, Joel spotted a familiar tree, one with a shape that had made him smile when he'd first seen it. He'd never been sure whether the trunk had split in two very early on, or whether two trees had grown close together, giving the impression they were one. Ivy grew up the middle, linking the two as they'd reached for the sun.

"Interesting-looking tree," Marcus said.

"Yeah. It reminds me of a relationship, of two people doing their own thing but linked by their love for each other." Joel crouched in front of it, checking the grass wasn't too wet before he sat.

Marcus studied the tree for a moment. "I like that analogy. It's also a good description of what I've always thought a relationship should be, but—" He smiled and joined Joel to sit on the grass, watching the stream. "—not forgetting the importance of finding time to be together, of course."

"Of course." Joel rested his head on Marcus's shoulder. "I've never told anyone about that before. It seemed... a little silly putting all that meaning on a tree."

"Sometimes," Marcus said slowly, "nature is good at reminding us about what's important. It's one of the reasons I like working outdoors. I enjoy the hard work, but it also gives me time to think, and often I'll see something like your tree that helps me put things in perspective."

"Yeah. That's why I like coming here to think." Joel picked up a tiny stick and turned it over in his hand. "I'm sorry I was quiet before. Mum thinks I need to be the one to break the silence between me and Dad."

"What do you think?"

"It's been sixteen years." Joel shrugged. "He's had a long time to come around. He's my father. Parents are supposed to love their kids, no matter what. We used... I thought... I used to... I still love him. I miss him. When I was a kid, I'd go to work with him on a Saturday afternoon after I finished playing soccer. At one point I seriously thought about learning his business and us working side by side."

"What happened?" Marcus asked softly.

"I... I don't know. I grew up, I guess, and realised my dad didn't know everything, I pursued my love for music, and decided to follow my own path, not his. And then I figured out I was gay, and..." Joel had already told Marcus about what happened next. God, he was tired of all of it. "The day I told my father I was gay was horrible."

"I can only imagine what that was like."

"I felt like the bottom had dropped out of my world. Nothing was what I thought it should be. It made me second-guess *everything*. I'd thought Dad would react the same way your parents did." Joel felt tears well at the memory. He scrubbed at his face. "I thought... I thought he loved me."

"I'm so sorry." Marcus wrapped his arm around Joel and ran his fingers through Joel's hair in a soothing motion. "I wish you hadn't had to go through that." He stared out at the water. A sudden gust of wind scattered leaves across its surface. "I can't believe your dad doesn't love you. I... Maybe he didn't know what to do, or how to deal with your being gay? My parents suspected I was, so maybe that helped."

"I don't know." Joel bit his lip. "I should be over this. I thought I was over it all. But now..." He couldn't hide the desperation he felt any longer. "His health is going to crap. What if something happens, and I never told him I still love him?"

"One of you needs to break the ice between you." Marcus stated the obvious.

Joel yanked free of Marcus's embrace, stood, and then started to pace. "Don't you think I know that? He's not going to, but... I can't. I just can't. What if I try and he won't? At least I still have the illusion he might have. But what if...?"

"At least if you talk to him, you'd know for sure."

"I'm not sure I want to know." Joel stalked over to the edge of the stream and threw the stick he held into the water. He picked up another, a bigger one, and threw that in as well, barely missing a duck swimming past. "I... Oh hell." He wrapped his arms around himself.

He wouldn't cry. He wouldn't cry. He wouldn't...

Marcus pulled Joel back into a firm embrace. "It's okay," he whispered. "I've got you. I'm not going anywhere. I'm here for you."

Joel turned to face Marcus. "I… I know. I believe you." He buried his head against Marcus's chest and let go—not only of how he was feeling now, but of the years of anger and grief he'd bottled up for so long. He didn't make any noise, yet his shoulders heaved in silent sobbing.

Marcus stroked Joel's back and continued to hold him tightly. "There's no one here but us. It's okay."

Joel didn't know how long they stood there, but when he finally looked up at Marcus again, he whispered, "Take me home." He felt exhausted, as though he had nothing left. He was tired, so tired, of all of this. "Can you stay with me?"

"I'll stay for as long as you need me." Although Marcus had said the words before, this time Joel knew he truly meant them.

Any lingering fear about Marcus's lack of commitment to their relationship had disappeared as Joel had sobbed in Marcus's arms.

"I *do* need you." Joel managed a shaky smile, tilted his head, and kissed Marcus long and slow. "Thank you."

Marcus slipped from the bed, making sure not to disturb Joel, who was still sleeping. After they'd finished talking, Joel was exhausted to the point he'd stumbled before they'd reached the car and nearly tripped on the curb. Back at Joel's house, Marcus tried to convince him to sleep for a while.

Joel had muttered something about needing to work, but Marcus finally persuaded him to rest by promising he'd stay with him until he drifted off to sleep. He wasn't planning to go too far afterwards either, but for now he needed to be doing something so he could work through everything Joel had told him.

Marcus leaned in to brush his lips against Joel's cheek.

Joel didn't stir. He looked peaceful in sleep, all the worry lines smoothed over, his tears long dried. Joel hadn't slept well for a while, so Marcus would let him rest until dinner, and then cook a decent meal to make sure he ate properly. They'd planned to watch *The Frighteners* together that evening. It would be a relaxing way to finish a stressful day.

While he drank his coffee, Marcus bent down to pat Nannerl. "You're hungry, aren't you?" She'd snuggled into Joel on the other side of the bed but then followed Marcus out to the kitchen when he got up. He wasn't surprised, though, that once she'd eaten, she brushed up against him for another pat and went back to be with Joel.

The drizzle stopped while he was tending to Joel and Nannerl, and the grey sky returned to blue. It was cooler now, but not enough to warrant a jersey. Marcus set aside his plan to tackle the lawns—the grass was too wet from the rain. However, it was the perfect weather for gardening, and pulling weeds would give him the chance to think without the risk of disturbing Joel with the noise of the mower.

He hated seeing Joel so upset.

Marcus stabbed at a particularly stubborn groundsel stem, digging around its roots until he was able to free it from the ground. Joel's miniature roses were tangled up in weeds, but that didn't stop the hardy little things from growing. Marcus sat back in a crouch and took a moment to breathe in their scent.

Shit, he wished he could fix this situation with Joel and his dad. Joel was right. Sixteen years wasn't something easily sorted out, and it would only get worse unless something changed. Joel wasn't simply upset by his father's illness; he missed the relationship they'd once had and worried that his final memories of his father would be of his disapproval and anger.

How could someone turn their back on Joel? The guy

cared about everyone he felt responsible for, maybe a bit too much. Marcus wasn't stupid. He'd figured out very quickly why Joel worked so hard. He wanted everything to be as good as it could be, not just for himself, but for the kids he taught. Yet, for a guy who took on responsibility for so much, he'd run from the one thing he never should have turned his back on.

Marcus sighed. He wasn't exactly one to talk. His relationship with Garth showed that loud and clear. The trouble with letting something slide for so long was that it made it next to impossible to backtrack and fix it later.

This situation wasn't totally Joel's fault. While Marcus could see Jill's concern for her husband and son, she'd left it almost too late. Marcus wasn't sure he would have been brave enough to do what Jill was attempting. She could clearly see the wall between father and son, but like them, didn't know how to dismantle it.

Perhaps Claude Ashcroft, like Joel, felt he couldn't take the first step. Even if he'd now realised he'd made a mistake, admitting that and doing something about it were very different things.

"Hello." Mavis called to Marcus from over the fence. She wore a look of concern, so he hoped she hadn't been calling him for a while.

He stood and walked over to her. "Good afternoon. I hope you're keeping well."

"Very well, and thanks for the great job you're doing with my lawns. I've told a few friends about you and given them your contact details. I hope that's okay."

"That's fine—and thank you. I appreciate it." Marcus glanced down when Nannerl rubbed against him. Once he'd noticed her, she sat down next to his gardening tools and started washing herself. He frowned. Why wasn't she with Joel?

In answer to his question, he heard piano music coming from the house. Joel must have woken and started practicing the prelude he was playing for the concert. So much for taking the afternoon off, although he had said a few times that he found it relaxing to play.

"Joel's very good, isn't he?" Mavis asked, yet it sounded more like a statement than a question. "I often hear him playing when I'm in my garden, although I haven't heard anything for a few months apart from that tune he's playing now. I had hoped I'd missed it because I've been out, rather than because he'd given up. Talent like his should be nurtured, don't you think?"

"Yes. He is very good." Marcus glanced at his watch. He'd been gardening for an hour, his thoughts distracting him for a good amount of that time. Good thing he did a lot of this kind of work on autopilot. Nevertheless he double-checked to make sure he hadn't targeted anything that wasn't a weed. He stood back to take a better look and smiled, satisfied with a job well done.

"You've been working hard." Mavis nodded approvingly. "If I get to the point where I can't do my own gardening, I'll keep you in mind."

"Thanks. I should probably head inside. It's been nice talking with you again."

"I'd hoped to catch you at some point so I could thank you for your work in person." Mavis handed him a small basket. "I've made some muffins and thought you and Joel might enjoy some."

"Thank you, that's very kind of you." Marcus was surprised by her generosity.

Mavis smiled. "It's the neighbourly thing to do. I've kept an eye on Joel for some time now, as he does work so very hard." She lowered her voice. "It's lovely seeing the two of you together and knowing he's got someone like you looking out for him when he gets caught up in things and works *too* hard. Sometimes you have to help people who don't help themselves, you know?"

Marcus wasn't sure how to reply to that. Joel hadn't been kidding when he'd said that Mavis knew everything that went on in their neighbourhood. "Thanks," he said again. "When is the best time to return the basket?"

"Leave it on my front doorstep. Goodness me, it is late. I'd better go fix dinner. Bye, Marcus."

"What's up?" Darin glanced out from under the bonnet of the car he was working on. After one look at Marcus, Darin wiped his grease-covered hands on an old towel and gestured towards his office. "We can talk in here where it's more private. Time I took a break anyway."

"I'm that obvious, huh?" Marcus hadn't had the chance to say more than hello before Darin presumed something was on his mind.

"Yeah, a bit. You've got that look Ella gets when she wants to talk about something she really *doesn't* want to talk about." Darin poured them both a coffee, handed one to Marcus, and took a seat on one of the office chairs.

Darin's workshop wasn't as big as others Marcus had seen, but since Darin bought the garage, he'd built up a decent-size customer base. His reputation as a motor mechanic who provided excellent service at reasonable prices had spread quickly. A couple of years ago, he'd bought the storage facility next door and converted it into more workspace. He'd also hired another mechanic and taken on an apprentice.

"Joel's working late to get ahead because of Nancy's birthday party tomorrow night, so I figured this was a good time to come talk to you." Marcus pulled the other chair closer to Darin so he wouldn't have to raise his voice to be heard. "Have you ever met Joel's father?"

"Yeah, but I haven't seen him since he and Joel stopped talking. Why? Did something happen?"

"No, but that's the problem." Marcus sipped his coffee while he collected his thoughts. "Joel's dad isn't in the best of health, but neither he nor Joel will back down and make the first move to mend their relationship."

"That's not surprising." Darin stirred another sugar into his coffee. "There's nearly sixteen years of history there. Have you tried talking to Joel about it?"

"He's talked to me about it, but…" Marcus sighed. He wasn't in a hurry to see Joel so upset again, although he suspected if something happened to Claude, Joel would never forgive himself.

"He has?" Darin raised an eyebrow. "He never talks to anyone about that shit. Not even me." Darin licked coffee off his spoon and then blew on his cup to cool it down. "So… I'm not sure I can do anything. I've suggested Joel talk to his dad before now, but after the first few times I gave up. Joel's more like his dad than he wants to admit."

"They're both stubborn?"

"Yeah, as hell." Darin took a sip of coffee. "Claude always struck me as a decent kind of guy. I was shocked when he and Joel fell out. I'd thought he'd be more understanding, and he always seemed to dote on Joel. The two of them had a good relationship before then."

"Do you think there's a chance he might come round, then?"

"He might, but I wouldn't guarantee it. And he's the one who owes Joel an apology, which doesn't help." Darin looked thoughtful. "Nothing's going to happen while the two of them keep avoiding each other."

"Joel's mum asked him to talk to his dad."

"Seriously? She's actually admitting there's a problem? Jill's a nice lady, but she'd run a mile to avoid conflict. She must be really worried even to mention it."

"I think so too. I suspect Joel wants to fix the relationship, but…" Although Marcus was talking to Darin about this stuff, he didn't want to say too much. If Joel wanted Darin to know the details, he'd talk to him about it himself.

"He's scared his dad will reject him again?" Darin guessed what Marcus hadn't said.

"I would be if I were him," Marcus said cautiously, not wanting to confirm or deny it. He took a deep breath. "I'm wondering… Neither of them is going to make the first step, and if his dad's health takes a turn for the worse before… What do you think about me going to talk to Claude?"

Darin let out a low whistle. "It might work, but Joel's not going to be happy if he finds out. Do you want to take that risk?"

"If I tell him I'm going to do it, he'll ask me not to. We're finally getting to the point of trusting each other with the stuff that really matters, and I don't want to screw that up." Marcus drained his coffee and wrapped his fingers around his cup. "But I can't help thinking he needs this sorted. It's eating him inside. If something happened, and I could have done something to help…"

"You really care about Joel, don't you?" Darin studied Marcus so intently he felt like squirming in his seat. "I mean, *really* care about him. This is more than friendship and great sex, isn't it? I know how difficult you find it to talk to anyone about the stuff that really matters. And aside from that, it's going to take a lot of courage to approach someone you don't know."

"I… I'm in love with Joel." Marcus blew out a loud breath.

It was the first time he'd said the words aloud to anyone, including himself.

"For what it's worth, I think it's mutual, but I'm guessing he probably hasn't told you either."

Marcus shrugged. "We both have a not-so-great history with relationships. I wanted to take this one slow, but it hasn't exactly worked out that way."

"I noticed." Darin put his empty coffee cup down on top of a pile of coffee-ringed papers. "I figured you're both old enough to know what you want. Why be lonely when you've found someone you want to be with?"

"Right." Marcus had told himself the same thing several times over. "Thing is, though, even if he does love me, is it enough to save what we have when he finds out I've talked to Claude?"

"Sometimes what you need isn't what you want," Darin said slowly. "Have you talked to Ella about this? It's not me you usually have these kinds of conversations with."

"I figured you knew Joel better."

"You know about Reed, right?" Darin asked. "That guy had a tendency to plan everything for both of them and expected Joel to go along with it."

"Yeah, I know about Reed," Marcus said cautiously. He wasn't sure how much Joel had told Darin about why they'd split up. "I'm not Reed," he said firmly.

"I know you're not. Reed was an arsehole. I was never sure what Joel saw in the guy, but he seemed happy, so I let it go. If I see him again, though, I'll tell him what I think."

"My priority is Joel. I don't *want* to talk to his dad. In fact, I'd prefer not to." Now Marcus wasn't sure what he should do.

"If you're not sure, that's probably a sign you shouldn't, at least not yet. But if that changes, for whatever reason, I say go for it. Otherwise, if something happens to Joel's father, you'll have to pick up the pieces."

"I'll think on it. Thanks." Marcus turned at the knock at the door.

"Darin, you got a minute?" One of the mechanics—his name tag said Larry—opened the door and poked his head around it. "I need you to talk to a customer."

"The Subaru?" Darin sighed when Larry nodded. "Figures. Thanks, I'll be there in a minute."

"Thanks for listening." Marcus stood.

"Hope it helped, and you're welcome to drop by anytime." Darin retrieved a clipboard from a hook on the wall by his desk. "Whatever you decide, I'll support you, okay?" A loud male voice yelled something nearby. Darin winced. "I need to go. Catch you later." He grinned. "Good to see Joel's got someone else looking out for him."

"Always," Marcus said, standing back to let Darin out of the small room. While talking to Darin had helped, Marcus still wasn't sure what he should do.

He hoped time would tell.

CHAPTER TWELVE

Joel had introduced Marcus to everyone when they'd arrived at the birthday party, then someone Joel knew greeted him with a hug and the conversation had quickly moved on to something about music. Marcus suspected they weren't talking about anything complex, but after only recognising every other word, if that, he'd given up trying to follow it. Finally, he'd brushed Joel lightly on the shoulder, mouthed something about getting a beer, and left them to it.

Marcus looked up when Toni, Nancy's wife, slid into the empty spot on the sofa.

"Another beer, or are you the designated driver tonight?" she asked.

"We're calling a taxi to take us home at the end of the evening," Marcus said. "How's it going? I thought you'd be the centre of the party, as it's your birthday."

While everyone was friendly enough, they weren't a group Marcus would have normally mixed with. He was quite content, though, to watch the proceedings from his spot on the sofa. Joel had finally started to unwind and sounded happy as he caught up with people he'd obviously known for some time. Every so often he'd glance over at Marcus to check that he was all right, and Marcus would reply with a smile and subtle thumbs up.

The atmosphere felt comfortable and relaxed. Men and women sat or stood in small groups around the living room, with some spilling out into the adjoining kitchen and hallway. The house was old, yet well maintained, the walls decorated with photographs and paintings of local scenery and musicians. A piano stood in one corner, the top piled high with sheet music, the bookcase next to it overflowing. Soft background music—jazz rather than classical, Joel had told Marcus with a grin—added to the ambiance.

Joel fit here, and it showed. Marcus felt more like an outsider. He hoped that would change the longer he and Joel were together, although he doubted he'd ever feel quite as at home in the music scene as Joel did. Despite it being Joel's passion, Marcus didn't feel the urge to embrace it in the same way. He was content to watch and listen.

"I'm mingling. As it's my birthday party, it's the responsible thing to do." Toni took another sip from the wineglass she held. "Besides, I hear the teacher gossip all day, so I wanted a rest from it. I'm glad you came with Joel. I wanted to meet you, especially after Nancy told me you'd been coming to a lot of Joel's rehearsals."

"I noticed most of the people here are teachers, musicians, or both." Marcus had never been one for social mingling and the only people he knew at the party were Joel and Nancy. Joel had told him that Nancy had painted several of the artworks he'd admired when they'd arrived. Her true passion was her art—and her wife—and she referred to her work at the school office as her "day job."

"I hope we're not too scary."

Toni smiled, although Marcus hadn't taken her comment seriously.

"Terribly," he said, deadpan. "Really, I'm glad we came—I was curious to meet more of Joel's friends, and he needed a break from work. Nancy's invitation came at the right time."

"A lot of people still don't get that teachers work long hours outside the time spent in front of the kids in the classroom." Toni wrinkled her nose, and Marcus laughed. He could see why she and Joel had been friends for a long time. She had a contagious bubbly personality. "Five years until I retire. It's going to be weird; Teaching has been a part of my life for so long. I love it, though."

"You'll continue conducting the kids' orchestra?" Marcus asked.

"Yeah. I'll be able to enjoy it more without having to squeeze it in amongst everything else." Toni caught Nancy's eye from across the room and gave her wife a wink. "More time for jazz gigs too. Sometimes I get to the end of the week and fall over, or I would, if I didn't have Nancy to hold me up." She balanced her glass on the arm of the sofa. "I was pleased when I heard Joel had found someone. He looks happier than he has in a long time, although it's been five years since he and Reed split up. Nancy and I are both sure you'll be better for him than Reed was. I was happy when Joel finally put his foot down and refused to go to Australia with him. That guy had got his own way for far too long. I was worried that Joel would lose himself if they stayed together."

"I'm happy with him too." The more Marcus heard about Reed, the less he liked the guy.

Joel laughed at something Nancy said to him and glanced over at Marcus. Marcus smiled. Joel ducked his head and blushed. Nancy giggled.

Toni gave Nancy a thumbs-up. "My Nancy likes to tease, and Joel has always blushed very well."

"Umm, yes, he..." Marcus thought about how sexy Joel

looked when that blush covered his *entire* body and stopped himself in time.

Toni laughed. "I get it. And for the record, you do as well." She sounded delighted. "Nancy will be pleased."

"Hey."

"Just joking," Toni reassured him. "I think I'm needed. Do you want me to send someone over to keep you company? Some people here need to be reminded not to talk shop." She collected her glass and skipped across the room, only stopping when a younger man caught her elbow.

Marcus started to tell her he was fine, but she'd already gone. A couple of moments later, Joel weaved his way through the other partygoers and headed Marcus's way.

"Enjoying the party?" Joel sat down beside Marcus and kissed him on the cheek. He smelt like beer and the aftershave he'd sprinkled on liberally before they left home. Marcus wouldn't have thought the two scents would work together, but when he leaned in and kissed Joel properly, his overriding sense of Joel drowned out everything else.

"Yeah. Toni's nice." Marcus shuffled over so Joel could snuggle in properly. Joel seemed relaxed tonight and happy to be close. "Looks like you're doing a fair bit of catching up."

"It's been a while since I've seen some of this crowd. We don't meet that often, but when we do, it's like no time has passed." Joel slipped his hand into Marcus's. "I went to uni with a few of them. Others joined our group along the way, like Toni and Nancy."

"You look like you fit here." Marcus caressed Joel's hand with his thumb.

Laugher accompanied a flurry of activity in the far corner. Someone turned the music off, and Marcus heard the sound of a violin being tuned. The man who had talked to Toni earlier started to play a slow waltz. He was soon joined by Toni on the flute, and another man on the piano.

Couples took to the floor and started to dance. Joel turned to Marcus. "Do you want to dance?"

"Sure." Marcus let Joel pull him to his feet and then wrapped his arms around Joel's waist. Joel leaned into him, and they began moving in time with the music. Joel sang softly along with it, and Marcus smiled.

Time seemed to slow as they danced together, and Marcus's universe shrank to him and Joel. Having Joel in his arms felt so right, and already he couldn't imagine a life without him in it.

"I love you," Joel murmured. He met Marcus's gaze when Marcus stilled and leaned his forehead against Joel's. "Come home with me tonight." Joel brushed his fingers against Marcus's cheek. "Not just for tonight, I mean. Move in with me."

Marcus's mouth felt dry. "I love you too," he whispered, "and yes, please. I'd like that. A lot."

Joel reached for the phone, half asleep. He sat bolt upright when he heard his sister's voice. "Bernie? What's wrong?"

"It's Dad." Bernie was crying. "He's gone. You're too late. I'm sorry. You're too late."

"What?" Joel's heart sped up. His skin felt clammy. "Too... late?"

"Too late." A man stood in the shadows by the curtains, an indistinct shape out of reach.

"Dad?" Joel pushed back the bedclothes and struggled to his feet. "Dad?" He glanced over to where he'd heard his father's voice, but there wasn't anything there. "Dad!"

"Joel, wake up." Marcus sounded worried. "Joel!"

Joel took another step towards where he'd been sure his

father had stood, torn between the man he sought and one who now held him. "Let go," he yelled. "Let go."

Then suddenly he was still in bed and in Marcus's arms. *But how? What?*

Joel shivered. "Marcus?"

"You had a bad dream." Marcus held Joel as though he never wanted to let go. "You... you were calling for your father."

"Yeah." Joel wrapped himself around Marcus. "A bad dream. I guess that was it." He frowned. "My phone..."

Marcus relaxed his grip enough to lean over Joel to grab his phone off the bedside table. "No calls or texts. It's fine." He showed Joel the phone and then returned it to the table. "Do you want to talk about it?"

"I..." Joel had been waking at night for weeks now, grasping at dreams that slipped through his fingers too quickly to know what they'd been about. Had they been about his father too?

But why today? He had been so happy that evening. He and Marcus had sat up late making plans for moving in together, and Marcus had repeated the words—*I love you*—when they'd made love before drifting off to sleep in each other's arms.

"Why don't I make us some tea? We can talk for a bit before we go back to sleep," Marcus suggested.

"Okay. Sorry I woke you."

"Don't ever apologise for that. Stay here and keep warm. I won't be long." Marcus pulled on his pyjama bottoms and sweatshirt and headed out the bedroom door.

Less than a moment after he'd gone, Nannerl ran into the room and jumped onto the bed. She strode over to Joel and head-butted him, demanding attention. Usually she slept on the bed between them, but tonight she'd stayed in her spot in front of the still-warm heater when they'd gone to bed. She always seemed to know when Joel was upset. He stroked her soft fur and started to calm, although he glanced across the room at the shadows in the corner.

He switched on the bedside lamp. It didn't banish the memories of what he'd seen or rid the room of its shadows.

It had been only a dream, hadn't it?

Joel shivered and shuffled onto Marcus's side of the bed. The sheets still felt warm. Not only that, but they smelt of him. The sense of Marcus's presence made him feel safe. Joel laid his head on Marcus's pillow and breathed in deeply.

I love you. Marcus's words replayed in Joel's mind. He clung to them, taking refuge in the knowledge that Marcus truly cared for him and wouldn't throw the sentiment away later.

His dream wasn't real. He'd talk to Marcus and confront it for the illusion it was.

"Do you want to keep my pillow?" Marcus asked when Joel took the pillow with him as he returned to his side. He gave Joel both mugs of tea to hold while he climbed into bed.

"No, it's fine. You can have it back." Joel didn't need it now that Marcus was there. He waited until Marcus was comfortable and propped up on the returned pillow, and then handed him his tea.

Marcus sipped his tea and waited for Joel to speak.

Nannerl glared at the human who had usurped her spot and retreated to the end of the bed to keep a close eye on both of them.

"I dreamed about Dad," Joel admitted. "The phone rang, and Bernie said he'd gone. She kept saying I was too late."

"I'm so sorry." Marcus swapped his cup to his other hand and wrapped his free arm around Joel.

"I thought I saw him." Joel bit his lip and gestured towards the corner. "He told me I was too late as well. I called to him, and..." He closed his eyes, dimly aware of

Marcus taking his tea from him and putting both cups on the bedside table.

"Shh, it's okay." Marcus held Joel and stroked his hair.

"I'm sorry." Joel wiped his eyes. "I thought I was over all this crap, that I'd made my peace." Not remembering his dreams meant they hadn't been important, or so he'd figured. Talking to Marcus about it that day by the stream had given him a sense of peace. However, it appeared his subconscious had finally stripped away the façade and showed his state of mind for what it truly was.

Crap. Why couldn't he get on with his life after taking a healthy dose of denial like others seemed to?

"This isn't your first nightmare," Marcus said softly. "I've heard them before, and you haven't been sleeping for weeks. I'm worried about you."

"I'll be fine."

Joel sighed. He didn't know how to talk about what was bothering him. He'd keep busy and distracted, and the issues with his father would go back to being where they belonged —locked away with the bad memories he didn't want to deal with yet.

"Perhaps you need to talk to your father," Marcus suggested.

"So he can remind me how much he loves me?" Joel snorted, then regretted his reaction when Marcus winced. "Don't you think I've thought about it?" He'd dialled his father's number once but hung up when Claude answered.

"You don't need to do it alone." Marcus kept stroking Joel's hair. "I can come with you."

"I don't think that's a good idea." Joel didn't want Marcus to be on the receiving end of his father's bigotry.

"One of you needs to start talking." Marcus didn't seem to want to let go of the idea. "Before it *is* too late."

"I don't want to think about that now." Joel cringed when he heard the dismissive tone in his voice.

"Please. I'm worried about you. If you won't talk to him, maybe I could—"

"Whatever." Joel retrieved his cup and drained his tea, dismissing the conversation. "Can we go back to sleep now? I'm tired."

"Okay." Marcus ignored his tea, turned out the light, pulled the blankets around both of them, and then spooned around Joel.

"I'm sorry," Joel whispered. "I just can't."

"It's okay." Marcus kissed the nape of Joel's neck. "I love you. You know that, right?"

"Yeah, I do. I love you too."

"I'm sorry, but we don't have any jobs going at present." The woman at the front desk smiled at Marcus apologetically. She appeared to be in her forties, so about ten years older than him, and her demeanour was friendly and open. "But if you give me your name and contact details, I can let you know if that changes."

"I'm not here to apply for a job. I'd like a word with Mr Ashcroft, if that's possible." Marcus had thought about phoning for an appointment but didn't want to take the chance that Claude might know who he was and refuse to see him. That might still happen, but Marcus figured it was harder to say no to someone's face.

Bernadette had mentioned that her father would be at his office on Mondays and Fridays, which worked well because Joel would be at the school and there was less risk of him spotting Marcus's SUV parked outside Ashcroft Engineering. Not that Joel ventured far from either school or home of late, but Marcus didn't want to push his luck. Marcus had been surprised when he'd discovered that the company's offices were only about half an hour from where Joel lived, rather than closer to his parents' home in Tawa.

"Mr. Ashcroft is a busy man." Hillary—according to the name plaque on her desk—peered at him closely. "Is it about a job in progress? Or one under contract?"

"No, it's about a personal matter." Marcus hadn't come all this way to give up that easily. At least she hadn't said that Claude wasn't in. It was a start. "Please. It's important." He took a deep breath. "I need to talk to him about his son."

Hillary raised an eyebrow, yet got up from her desk immediately. "Wait here. What did you say your name was, again?"

"I didn't." Marcus's heart hammered in his chest. "You can tell him Marcus Verden is here to see him."

Not that Claude would know who he was, but perhaps that was a good thing. If he knew Marcus was Joel's boyfriend, he might refuse to see him.

Hillary's expression softened. "I'll see what I can do." She hesitated before she knocked on the office door. "Joel's all right, isn't he?"

Marcus nodded. How did Hillary know Joel's name? Did Claude still talk about his son? Or had she found out about Joel from someone else?

He debated sitting while he waited, then decided he'd prefer to stand. He wanted to meet Claude for the first time eye to eye, and not give the older man any advantage. This wasn't going to be easy, but Marcus was determined to say what he needed before he got thrown out. At least then he'd know he'd tried.

Looking around the room while he waited didn't prove to be the distraction he'd hoped for. The decor was a tasteful off-white, with a painting of the Kelburn cable car overlooking Wellington city adding colour to one wall. The floors were wood, possibly rimu, and polished with wax rather than painted with polyurethane—Marcus wondered if they'd been retrieved from a building site or part of the original building, which looked as though it had once been an old house.

It seemed like forever before Hillary came out of the office, giving Marcus time to examine his surroundings in detail at least twice. Marcus had heard voices, but they were too low to make out Claude's response.

"He'll see you now." Hillary smiled as Marcus gave her a curt nod and wiped his damp hands on his jeans. "He's surprised you're here, but he relaxed once he knew Joel was okay." She chuckled. "You look a lot like your sister, Marcus, and Joel's mother has given you her seal of approval, so remember that when you talk to Mr Ashcroft."

"Thanks." Marcus wondered—not for the first time—if anything happened in the Hutt Valley that his sister didn't know about. Ella had always believed in the power of networking, but discovering how many people knew her was getting surreal.

When Marcus entered the room, Claude Ashcroft stood and walked around to the front of his huge old-fashioned wooden desk to shake Marcus's hand. "Take a seat please, Marcus," he said, indicating one of two comfortable-looking leather loveseats on either side of a small coffee table. "Let's make this as easy as we can."

"Thank you, sir." Marcus took care to keep his tone polite, but he'd been curious about Claude for some time. While Joel had talked about his father, he'd never described him, and the only family photographs he had on display were of his mother, Bernadette, and Bernadette's family.

Claude was a few centimetres taller and more heavily built than Joel. He'd gripped Marcus's hand firmly, the calluses on his hands betraying his working man's background. Marcus sat on one sofa, while Claude took the other. Claude studied him in much the same way Marcus was watching him.

"I've been told Joel is a mix of me and his mother." Claude broke the silence with a comment that suggested he'd guessed what Marcus had been thinking. "I can't see it, but…" He shrugged, his lips turning up into a familiar smile.

"I can," Marcus said quietly. "I'd recognise that smile anywhere. It reminds me of Joel." Joel often wore it when he was nervous, but instead of talking about anything and everything, Claude accompanied it with a sense of quiet contemplation.

"So, you're Ella's brother?" Claude poured himself a glass of water from the pitcher on the table. He offered Marcus one, but Marcus shook his head. "I was surprised when I heard she and Bernie were friends, but I shouldn't have been, considering she married the Prior boy. I was glad Darin and Joel remained close. I knew he'd look out for my son."

Marcus wasn't sure how to take that statement. Surely if Claude was that worried about Joel, he'd do something about making sure he was all right himself. "Yes, Ella's my sister," he said cautiously. "I, umm… I'm here because of Joel."

"I know why you're here, young man." Claude took a long sip of water and then pulled out a handkerchief and wiped his brow. "I really must ask Hillary to turn down the air conditioning." He folded his handkerchief and returned it to his pocket. "So, you're dating my son."

"We just moved in together, actually." Marcus didn't see the harm in telling Claude. If he knew who Marcus was, it probably wouldn't be long before whoever was keeping him updated passed along that information too.

"Does Joel know you're here?" Claude got right to the point.

"No." Marcus regretted refusing the water. At least he could have taken a sip to mask his growing nervousness.

"Good." Claude's smile vanished, although his comment suggested he was pleased by Marcus's answer. "So… how is he doing? Hillary told me you'd said Joel was okay, so it can't be anything serious. He's not working too hard with that concert coming up, is he?"

"You know about that?"

"Of course I do." Claude seemed surprised by Marcus's question. "Just because my son and I are… I might not have spoken to him directly, but that doesn't mean I don't make it my business to find out how he is. He's still my son, after all."

Marcus took a deep breath. There was no way of saying what he needed to without being blunt. "Perhaps you need to tell him that?"

"I'm presuming that you're here because he still doesn't want to talk to me." Claude phrased his words as a statement rather than a question.

"Do you blame him?" Marcus was careful not betray Joel's trust. It was one thing to come talk to Claude, yet quite another to tell him exactly how his son felt about the situation.

"How did your parents react when you told them you were gay?" Claude asked the question so quietly that Marcus almost missed it.

"They were supportive and accepted me for who I am." Marcus saw Claude wince, so added quickly, "They'd already suspected I was gay." Alienating Claude at this point wouldn't help.

"Parents don't always know the answers, and we make mistakes," Claude said softly. He let out a long sigh. "It's been a long time since Joel and I talked. The longer I left it, the harder it became." He shrugged. "I worry I've already left it too late."

"You haven't," Marcus said firmly.

Claude shrugged again. "You probably wonder why I'm talking to you about this. Sometimes it's easier to speak to someone you don't know about the things that matter." He smiled wryly. "I can already see what my son sees in you. You get to the point straightaway, and you're not afraid to say what needs saying. Joel always appreciated that."

"You owe your son an apology." Marcus wondered if he'd gone too far when his comment was met by silence.

"I was brought up to believe that… what he is was wrong," Claude said finally. "I'm still not sure I can support his choice of lifestyle."

Marcus opened his mouth to tell Claude that being gay wasn't a choice, but then he figured he was better off focusing on baby steps and one at a time. He studied a knot in one of the floorboards under the table instead.

"I want him to be happy." Claude said.

It appeared as though an apology wouldn't be in the cards, but at least Claude seemed open to the idea of talking to Joel.

"I think you're missing out by not being a part of Joel's life. He's a great guy." Marcus forced himself to meet Claude's gaze directly. "Don't tell me you want him to be happy. Tell *him*."

"I'll think about it." Claude stood, so Marcus did too. Apparently their conversation was finished. "Thank you for coming to see me." He shook Marcus's hand again. "You won't tell my son we've met, will you?"

"If he asks me, I won't lie to him." Marcus hoped Joel wouldn't ask, but whatever happened now, he didn't regret this meeting.

"Good answer." Claude gave him a nod. "Goodbye, Marcus. Take care of my son."

Marcus felt a knot in the bottom of his stomach. Had all

of this been a waste of time? He gave Claude a nod of his own. "Goodbye, sir. Thank you for listening."

He hadn't been thrown out, so perhaps with time, Claude might reconsider his stance and make a move. Marcus hoped so, because he doubted Joel would. Marcus had done what he could. The rest was up to Joel and Claude—two men who were obviously each as stubborn as the other.

CHAPTER THIRTEEN

Marcus looked up in surprise when Joel wandered into the kitchen, running his hand through his hair. "Sorry if I woke you," Marcus said. "I'd hoped to let you sleep."

It had been nearly a week since he'd talked to Claude, and so far nothing had come from it. Marcus hoped Claude might at least come to the concert, although he wasn't counting on it. Had speaking with him been a waste of time?

Joel yawned. "Is that coffee I smell?" He walked over to Marcus, slipped his arms around him, and rested his chin on Marcus's shoulder. "I'd set my alarm to go off in another ten minutes, but when I noticed you weren't there, I figured I might as well get up early." He kissed Marcus's neck.

"You could go back to bed and sleep." Marcus suspected he was wasting his time suggesting it.

"Sounds lovely, but I need to be out the door by nine." Joel yawned again, disentangled himself from Marcus, and retrieved a mug from the dishwasher.

"It's Saturday," Marcus pointed out. "Your day off. Or at least one of them." Marcus was working that morning but would be finished by one. "I'm taking you out to lunch, remember?"

"Yeah, I know. I'm looking forward to it too." Joel poured himself some coffee. "Nancy texted me last night after you went to bed. Toni's got that lurgy that's going around, so I'm taking her orchestra rehearsal this morning."

"What about all the work you have to do this weekend?" Marcus raised an eyebrow.

"Toni didn't want her kids to miss out, and I wouldn't want that either." Joel popped a couple of slices of bread in the toaster. "I'll work a bit later tonight. It's no biggie."

"Joel…" Marcus didn't want to start the weekend with an argument. "Okay, I can see why you'd want to do this for the kids, but promise me you'll look after yourself."

"I'm fine." Joel grabbed the jam from the refrigerator and looked around for the margarine.

Marcus took them off him. "I'll take care of your toast. Sit and drink your coffee." Joel opened his mouth to protest, took one look at Marcus's expression, and sat down.

"I'm fine," he repeated. "Still waking up, that's all."

"You didn't sleep again last night, and I can see bags under your eyes. You're going to be charged for excess luggage if you keep this up."

"Ha-ha." Joel stuck his tongue out. "Look, I can see you're worried, but don't be. Give me another three weeks, and I'll take a good-sized break. Promise."

"I am worried about you." Marcus sighed. "And yes, I know you warned me about this, but that doesn't mean I can't take care of you and stop you from replacing one lot of stress with another. Because you will, won't you?"

Joel shrugged. "You knew what you were signing up for. I'm sorry, but I have to get through this and out the other side. I appreciate your wanting to help, but I'm an adult. I know what I'm doing."

Marcus snorted. "This isn't just concert stress. Those bad dreams aren't going away either. Something's going to give if you don't slow down." The toaster popped. Marcus added the spreads to the toast and put the plate down in front of Joel. "Okay, what about this for an idea? You're filling in for Toni today, so why not ask her to take your kids for a rehearsal? You said it could help to get a second opinion about where they're at. You can take that evening off to catch up instead of working late tonight."

"Hmm." Joel took a bite of toast and chewed thoughtfully. "I think the pieces are coming together well, but what you said has possibilities. If Toni takes my orchestra rehearsal at the school one evening, I could fit in an extra practice for the choir and go over that bit they're still having issues with. Actually…" He looked up at Marcus. "What? You don't agree?"

Marcus took several deep breaths and reminded himself that he loved Joel and how passionate Joel was about what he did. "You're not helping yourself in the slightest," he muttered. "I'm trying to get you to take a break." Marcus pinched the bridge of his nose. "You work too hard, and I'm already worried about you, without you taking on something else."

"You know that saying about if you want something done, you give it to a busy person."

"I don't remember there being a postscript saying it had to be you." Marcus wasn't going to win this, and he didn't want an argument. One last ditch attempt and he'd give up. "Just make sure you take breaks, okay? I don't want you getting that virus Toni's come down with. If you get sick now, all your work is for nothing."

Joel seemed to consider the concept. "Yeah, good point. Don't worry. I don't want to get sick. Look, I'm sorry we haven't got to spend much time together the last couple of weeks. I'll make it up to you once this is over. We've got that trip planned to Hokitika next school holidays. I'm looking forward to some time off and getting to know your parents better. I haven't seen them since the last time they were up here visiting Ella."

"I'm not worried about the amount of time we're spending together," Marcus told him. "I'm worried about *you.*"

Joel's expression softened. He drained the rest of his coffee. "I know. I'm not used to having someone looking out for me the way you do. I can't promise to slow down, but I'll try to be a bit more sensible." He pushed back his chair and walked over to Marcus.

Marcus smiled at Joel's determined expression. He brushed back the long locks of Joel's fringe and kissed him. "I do love you, you know, and I mean it when I say I want to be here for you, no matter what."

"I know. I love you too." Joel returned the kiss, and Marcus felt Joel's hardening erection pushing up against him. "Join me for a shower before we both head out?"

"Okay." Marcus kissed Joel again, this time cupping Joel's face with both hands. "I'd love to."

Joel closed his eyes. The notes on the page in front of him began to swim, the crotchets growing extra stalks as they merged into the quavers next to them.

Exhaustion had caught up with him, and he didn't have the energy fight to it. He'd intended to take Marcus's advice and ask Toni to fill in for him, but her illness had hit her hard, and Joel had ended up taking her rehearsals two Saturdays in a row on top of his own. Despite Adelaide cancelling her son's usual Friday lesson, Joel's vow to use the extra time to practise wasn't working out at all.

Why had he agreed to play at this bloody concert? He could manage the concert itself, but now it was only days away, he wondered what had possessed him to agree to perform and wave goodbye to his sanity.

The prelude had seemed doable at first. Joel had once enjoyed the adrenaline rush of a performance, and he loved playing in public before that terrible day when his dreams had crashed around him. Conducting was different. So was accompanying the choir. He got nervous doing that during performances too, but not like this.

His hands shook. Joel wiped them on his jeans. What was wrong with him? When he'd chosen this piece, he'd felt confident he could play it. But that was before most of the time he'd put aside to practise had been swallowed up by a balancing act of concert preparation and the already huge workload that accompanied his job.

He cleared his throat, ignoring the scratchy feeling when he swallowed. Damn it. He couldn't afford to get sick now. Did they still have some lemon and ginger tea? Joel couldn't remember whether he'd put it on the shopping list or not.

Halfway to the kitchen, he nearly walked into Marcus in the hallway. Marcus tucked the book he carried under one arm and led Joel to the kitchen. He often sat in the living room quietly reading while Joel practised or worked.

"Talk to me, and I'll make you a drink," Marcus suggested.

"Thanks. Lemon and ginger tea if we have it."

"Scratchy throat?" Marcus put the kettle on and sat down next to Joel while he waited for it to boil. "What else is up? Still worried about performing?"

"Yeah. I'm seriously considering not going ahead with it. I know the kids will be disappointed, but better that than make a complete cock-up of it. The concert's on Monday, so I only have this weekend left to practise."

"You'll be brilliant, I know you will." Marcus put his arm around Joel. "And if you make a mistake, it will show the kids that everyone does, so if they do it's no big deal either."

"Yeah, I suppose." Joel sighed and rubbed at his eyes. He couldn't remember the last time he'd had a decent night's sleep. "I'm fine when I play for just you, but as soon as I think about performing in front of all those people, I start making stupid mistakes. It's been too long since I've done this."

"I love listening to you play." Marcus sounded thoughtful. "Hmm, so do you think you could pretend you're only playing for me on the night? I could move just before you play so I'm standing where you can see me when you glance up from the piano. No one else needs to know but us."

"That might work." Joel loved playing for Marcus. It always felt like he was sharing a part of himself with Marcus that no one else saw, the vulnerable side of himself he trusted Marcus to keep safe no matter what. "I can pretend the rest of the hall doesn't exist."

"Perhaps for a while it won't, at least until everyone applauds when you're done." Marcus smiled, almost shyly. "Knowing you're playing just for me makes me feel all warm inside."

"I'll remember that." Joel would play for Marcus after this concert too, a private performance with candles, followed by another very personal thank-you for his support through all of this.

"So... what else is up?"

"You don't miss much, do you?" Joel looked down when sharp claws dug into his leg through his jeans. He petted Nannerl almost absently.

"I try not to." Marcus got up to make their drinks. He fed Nannerl some treats while he was at it. "Are you still worried about your dad? I heard you calling out for him again last night."

"Yeah, a bit I guess." Joel shrugged. He half expected the phone call of his nightmares, although Bernadette had told him their father seemed much better. "A couple of the kids asked me if you were my boyfriend. They've noticed you sitting in at a few of the rehearsals."

"What did you tell them?" Thankfully, Marcus didn't comment about Joel's obvious change of subject.

"That you were, of course." Joel chuckled at the memory. "One of those girls, the ones I told you were far more boy-focused than schoolwork-focused, told me she thought you were hot, and that we were cute together." He'd coloured at the time but hid it quickly.

"What did you tell her?" Marcus looked surprised.

"I wasn't going to lie to her." Joel took the hot mug from Marcus, their fingers brushing together and lingering. "I told her I thought you were too." He'd moved the subject along after that, not wanting to talk about personal things with a student. "I'm surprised it took the kids that long to ask me, actually. The fact I'm gay was around the school about five minutes after I told Adelaide you're my boyfriend. I guess they finally decided they wanted to confirm the rumours."

"It's important to do that, and it's good they don't believe everything they hear about people." Marcus shifted his chair so he was sitting next to Joel rather than across from him. He sipped his coffee slowly, a sure sign he was thinking. "Darin rang earlier and asked if we wanted to go for drinks tonight before dinner. I said I'd check with you first. Are you feeling up to it?"

"I'm not sick, just tired, and yeah that sounds good." Joel had turned down the offer the last few Fridays and spent the time working instead, although he'd made sure they weren't late for dinner. He didn't need Ella on his arse—she'd mother him and make Marcus's protective streak look like he was merely an apprentice.

"Have you thought again about talking to your dad?" Marcus's question took Joel by surprise. So much for Marcus letting him get away with the obvious change of subject.

"Yeah, I've thought about it, and the answer is still no." Joel slipped his hand into Marcus's and squeezed it. "Some things aren't meant to change," he said softly. "I've had months of nightmares about all sorts of stuff when I've worked this hard other times too. They'll settle down again once this concert is over. I promise."

In a perfect world, his father would come to this concert, and they'd talk again as though the years they'd lost had never happened. But there was no point in getting his hopes up for the impossible. Joel preferred to focus on what he did have—a relationship with a man he was crazy about and the rest of his family finally coming together to support him. His family had been Darin, Ella, and Isabel for so many years. He loved them to bits, but he'd found it difficult knowing his own family wasn't there when he needed them.

"Okay." Marcus didn't sound convinced. "You'll take the rest of tonight off, though, right? I thought we could come home and watch a movie or something. It's been a while since we've cuddled and drifted off to sleep on the sofa together. I've missed being woken up by your snoring on my lap."

"I do *not* snore," Joel said indignantly. He laughed and ducked his head when Marcus snorted.

"Do too." Marcus kept a straight face for all of a minute and then laughed. Joel grinned. He loved Marcus's laugh. It was infectious as hell.

"Yes, by the way."

"Yes?"

"To watching a movie and cuddling on the sofa after we

get home." Joel kissed Marcus's fingers. "Thanks for listening. I still feel nervous about playing, but a bit of that is a good thing."

"Anytime, and yeah I've heard that before." Marcus licked his lips, the action going straight to Joel's cock.

"I'll let Darin know we're on for tonight, but..." Joel reached for his phone and sent a text. "Neither of us will be ready for at least another half an hour. Sound good?"

"Very good." Marcus took the phone from Joel and placed it on the table. "I want you," he said in a low voice.

"Now." Joel pushed back his chair to let Marcus straddle him, their lips meeting in a breathtaking kiss. Marcus was right. A night off was exactly what Joel needed. What they both needed.

CHAPTER FOURTEEN

Adelaide Barker tapped the side of the microphone. A loud screeching noise filled the auditorium. Marcus jumped, though he'd half expected it. Next to him, Isabel giggled.

At first Marcus had thought Joel managed to get them front row seats, but Ella was to thank for it. Next to Darin an empty seat waited for Adelaide to finish her introduction. On the other side of it, Caleb Barker shuffled in his seat, giving a good impression of wishing he was somewhere else.

"Do you want to move next to me so you're not sitting alone?" Darin asked. "Your mum can take the seat you're in now."

"Thanks, Mr Prior." Caleb glanced at his mother and shifted seats quickly. He smiled at Darin, looking happier than he had sitting by himself.

Jill and Bernadette sat on Marcus's other side. There was another empty seat on Bernadette's right, next to the aisle, but so far no one had come to claim it.

"Welcome, everyone, to Avalon College's midyear fundraiser concert." Adelaide beamed at the audience. "We're delighted by the turnout, and we're sure you'll enjoy the evening. I'd like to thank Joel Ashcroft for all his hard work with the choir and orchestra. As a special treat, he's agreed to play a solo piano piece for us this evening."

The audience clapped politely. Marcus caught a glimpse of Joel peering around the curtain. He looked fabulous in his dark suit, and Marcus had bought him a bow tie for the occasion, the colour matching the shade of Joel's eyes perfectly. He'd been nervous earlier, his fingers shaking as he'd asked Marcus to help him with his tie.

"Remember you're playing for me," Marcus had whispered, giving Joel a kiss for luck.

Joel nodded and he'd hugged Marcus tightly. He'd been uncharacteristically quiet on the drive to the school. Marcus had offered to drive so it was one less thing for Joel to worry about. He didn't mind arriving early and had hung around backstage with Joel as long as he could before taking his seat when the doors opened and the auditorium quickly filled up.

"I'd also like to thank the PTA for all their hard work in making this evening possible. It's been a pleasure seeing my idea come to fruition," Adelaide continued.

Ella muttered something under her breath. Darin laid a hand on her arm and whispered something Marcus couldn't hear.

"But without any further words, I'll hand you over to our own Joel Ashcroft and the Avalon College choir." Adelaide smiled when Joel came out onto the stage. He gave her a small nod as he walked past her onto the podium in front of the choir.

Toni sat at the piano. She'd offered to accompany the choir for the evening to take some of the pressure off Joel. While he usually played for the choir, as these pieces were more intricate than usual, he figured they'd feel more confident having their conductor in front of them.

Joel bowed to the audience, smiling when his gaze settled

on Marcus who gave him a thumbs-up sign and mouthed the words "*I love you.*" Joel turned around to face the choir, then raised his baton.

Most of the students kept their eyes on Joel, although one girl kept looking at the audience as though trying to find someone. Joel glanced in her direction, and she gave him a shaky smile. The piece began in unison and then broke into parts—the choir sounded amazing, and their voices blended perfectly. Marcus recognised the song immediately—Joel had been listening to everything on the program on a continuous loop for weeks.

As the final strains of "Puttin' on the Ritz" finished, Joel lowered his baton and gestured for the choir to bow. The audience clapped loudly, showing their appreciation of the performance. The girl Joel had glanced at earlier still looked nervous, but she smiled along with the rest of choir. Joel said something to her in a low voice, and she giggled, her expression brightening immediately.

Joel turned to address the audience, again seeking out Marcus before he spoke. "Thank you for coming tonight. The students have worked very hard and I'm very proud of them. I hope you enjoy the rest of our concert." He paused. "Before we continue, I'd also like to thank my family, and in particular my partner. Even conductors get nervous, and knowing they're here tonight helps a lot. But, anyway, enough from me. You've come tonight to hear the choir, and I'm sure you'll recognise this next song."

He nodded to Toni, and she began to play once more. The choir began singing a Māori lullaby, "Hine e Hine," in unison. But when they split into two-part harmony a few moments later, the piano faded away and the choir continued a cappella.

The audience was completely silent while they listened, and some wiped tears from their eyes when the piece finished. Joel lowered his baton once more and motioned for the choir to take a bow. After they had, they retreated to the bench seats immediately behind them.

Joel walked over to the piano and gave Toni a brief side-hug before taking her place on the stool. He didn't introduce the Chopin prelude—he'd written something for the printed program about it so he wouldn't need to.

He placed his fingers on the keys, and froze, his expression strained, his body tense.

The audience grew quiet, waiting.

Joel scanned the audience, relaxing when he met Marcus's steady gaze.

I love you, Marcus mouthed. The seat Ella had given him allowed a perfect view of the piano. More importantly, it meant that Joel could see Marcus without anyone blocking his vision.

Joel managed a smile. He began to play.

Listening to the piece he now knew so well, Marcus could feel a sense of Joel's personality reflected in the music while he played. His mouth felt dry, as Joel gave his best performance of the prelude Marcus had ever heard. The music wasn't just a succession of notes, but when Joel poured his emotions into the piece, the dynamics brought it to life. Marcus would never forget the first time Joel had played the prelude for him, and hearing it never failed to remind him of their shared journey since then and the future he wanted with Joel. Their first kiss on that evening months ago had opened both of their hearts and led Marcus to the realisation that he loved Joel with everything he was.

Joel played the final notes and sat silently for a moment, still resting his fingers on the keyboard. When he stood to take his bow, Marcus stood too, clapping loudly. The audience behind him followed his example, filling the hall with applause.

Adelaide Barker took to the microphone again. "That was amazing, wasn't it?" She sighed. "We're so lucky to have him. Please join me in showing your appreciation again."

The audience burst into more applause, until Adelaide motioned for them to sit. Joel blushed bright red and ducked his head, clearly embarrassed by her comments.

"And that's halftime, everyone," she said. "Enjoy the supper in the room next door, and we'll be back for part two in twenty minutes."

Joel waited until the choir had left the stage and then made his way down the steps. Marcus met him partway and pulled him into a hug. "You were wonderful," he whispered. "I love you."

"I played that piece for you like you suggested," Joel said softly, "and I love you too. Thank you."

"You haven't lost your touch." Bernadette gave Joel a hug and then stood back to let their mother do the same. "That was awesome."

"What Bernadette said." Jill smiled and gave Joel a quick kiss on the cheek. "Congratulations. I'm so proud of you, and I think the choir sounds beautiful too. Bernadette and I are going to get a cup of tea and some supper. I'm sure some of the parents are waiting to talk to you. I'm looking forward to the second half of the program."

"Thanks, Mum. You too, Bernie." Joel slipped one hand into Marcus's for a moment and squeezed. He looked over Marcus's shoulder. "Mum's right. There are a few parents here. If you want to go grab a cuppa, I don't mind. After all, we've got the rest of the evening to celebrate, and there's still the second half to go."

Marcus glanced at the retreating forms of Joel's family and hesitated. While he wanted to stay with Joel, he didn't want to be in the way either, and he didn't know how many

of the parents knew that when Joel had referred to his partner, he'd meant a man.

He turned at the hand on his arm.

"Come and get some supper," Darin said. "Those parents
are going to swamp Joel for a bit, and then you can swoop in
and rescue him in a few."

"If you're sure," Marcus asked Joel.

Joel nodded. "Go grab some refreshments. I'm counting
on the swooping later, though." An older man pushed
through the crowd and began talking to Joel, edging him off
to the side. Joel glanced up at the podium and then began
talking to him.

Adelaide Barker stood behind one of the tables, pouring
cups of tea, coffee, and juice. Beside her, Ella waved to
Marcus when he approached. Marcus had wondered why
Adelaide hadn't attempted to push in and highjack Joel
herself, but being part of the PTA meant helping out with the
supper.

"Nice to see you here supporting Joel, Mr Verden," she
said brightly, handing him a cup of tea. "We're all very proud
of him, you know."

"So am I." Marcus took the tea but turned down her offer
of a piece of ginger slice to go with it, despite the fact she
told him she'd made it herself. He didn't feel hungry,
although neither he nor Joel had eaten much dinner.

Still no sign of Claude Ashcroft. Bernadette had told
Marcus they'd bought an extra ticket in case, but her father
had made his excuses and refused to come with them.

"Uncle Marcus." Isabel poked him in his side. "You're not
listening to me, are you?"

"I'm sorry, Issy." Marcus balanced his cup on his saucer. "I
was miles away."

Isabel giggled. "I noticed. Don't worry. I won't tell anyone
if you don't."

"Thanks." Marcus noticed she was frowning. "What's up? You're enjoying the concert, right?"

"Oh, yes. I think it's very good." Isabel lowered her voice like she was part of a conspiracy. "I need to go find my friends, but Dad said to tell you Uncle Joel needs rescuing now and that you should take him a cup of tea. He always forgets to take care of himself at these things."

"Okay, thanks." Marcus discarded his own cup, which he'd finished with anyway. "I'll get onto that now. Thanks. Talk to you later, okay?"

Ella handed him another cup of tea, this time in a mug, before he had the chance to ask for one. She grinned when he rolled his eyes. "Later."

"Yes, Mum," he replied and went off in search of Joel.

Joel hadn't moved very far from where Marcus had left him, but the throng of people surrounding him seemed to have grown exponentially. Marcus pushed through the throng with a few mumbled *excuse me*'s until he reached Joel's side.

"Your tea, sir."

Joel chuckled. "Thanks." He turned to the people around him. "It's been lovely chatting, but I need to take a break, so I can get through the rest of the performance. If you want to chat more, feel free to catch me after school. There won't be any rehearsals for choir or orchestra until next term, so that will make it easier."

"But I—" The woman who had been talking to Joel when Marcus arrived didn't appreciate Joel's attempt to end their conversation.

"The second half is starting in five minutes." Marcus stepped between her and Joel, but he made sure to keep his tone polite and his stance nonthreatening. "As Mr. Ashcroft said, he's available to chat with after school."

"Oh, I'm sorry. I didn't realise I'd taken up so much of

your time." She glanced at Marcus. "I don't think I've seen you at school. Are you a friend of Mr Ashcroft's? You must be very proud of him."

"Marcus is family, Mrs Hills," Joel said, "and it's fine. We're all caught up in the excitement of the evening. I'm sorry to cut you short, but we do need to get the second half underway or it's going to be a late night for the kids."

"Family?" asked Marcus after she was out of earshot. He'd noticed Joel hadn't introduced him as his boyfriend. Perhaps he wasn't as ready to be out at school as Marcus thought he was, despite his confirming the rumours he was gay. It was one thing for Adelaide and a few students to have found out, quite another to announce it to the world.

Joel shrugged. "Well, yeah. You're my partner. Same thing, right?" He drained his tea and handed Marcus the empty mug. "Like a knight, but without the horse and shining armour," he said dreamily.

"Huh?" Marcus wondered if Joel working too hard meant he had finally lost the plot, but Joel just grinned at him.

"Later. I need to get back to work." Joel paused. "You don't mind if I tell people who you are? Who you are to me, I mean."

"Of course not." Marcus smiled, his earlier doubts swept away. "This isn't my workplace, it's yours. But if you want people to know, I'm happy for you to tell them."

"Thank you." Joel ducked his head, a sign he was thinking about something.

"Always." Marcus headed off to return Joel's mug so he could retrieve his seat before the rest of the concert started. Whatever was going through Joel's mind, Marcus was sure he'd find out in time.

~

A few minutes after the warning that the second half was about to begin, the stragglers in the audience returned to their seats.

Joel waited for the students in the orchestra to take their places and their concertmaster to ask each section to tune their instruments. He'd made sure they already done it backstage, so repeating that now was for show and a part of the performance.

The orchestra stood as Joel walked out onstage. He shook hands with the concertmaster, and the orchestra sat again as Joel took his place on the podium. He lifted his baton, and the orchestra began to play Leroy Anderson's "The Syncopated Clock." After that, they went straight into their second performance—"The Radetzky March" by Strauss.

Applause thundered through the hall after Joel lowered his baton. The orchestral students all wore huge grins, and Joel gave them a thumbs-up. He turned to the audience to announce the final piece of the evening.

"Thank you. The orchestra has worked very hard, and I'm amazed by how far they've come since we began rehearsals." Joel scanned the audience, spotted Marcus, and smiled. He lifted his head, settling his gaze on the back of the auditorium before continuing to speak.

Oh God.

A chill ran up Joel's spine. Surely not... but... he took a deep breath. He caught Marcus's eye as Marcus turned to see what Joel was looking at.

Claude Ashcroft stood by the door. He smiled, but when Joel tried to catch his father's eye, he looked away.

Marcus turned back to Joel and mouthed, "Keep going. You're doing great."

Joel took a deep breath. He could do this. "I now invite the choir to come back onstage." He ignored the tremble in his voice and hoped no one had noticed.

What had felt like minutes must have been seconds as only Marcus seemed to notice Joel's hesitation. Joel shifted his attention away from his father to Marcus. He'd focus on Marcus and speak to him. He couldn't talk to his father now, as much as he wanted to, so that would have to wait for later. The kids had done so much work to prepare for the night's performance, and Joel couldn't let his personal problems interfere with that.

Once the choir had settled, Joel continued with his introduction. "I hope you enjoy this arrangement for choir and orchestra, and I'm sure you'll recognise the music." He turned and raised his baton, making sure that both choir and orchestra were ready.

As the orchestra began to play the opening bars of "A Whole New World," Joel found his nervousness dissolved with the music. He'd always loved that song, and he'd figured if he chose one the kids were familiar with, it would help them feel more confident.

When they finished, the applause was even louder. Joel turned to find some of the audience already on their feet. He felt warm inside and gestured for the students to take a bow with him.

From the edge of the stage, Adelaide called out, "Speech!" The sentiment was soon caught by others in the audience, and Joel found himself in front of the microphone once more.

Joel glanced up at the back of the auditorium, but his father was gone. Joel frowned, yet a quick visual search confirmed it. Had he been hoping so much for his father to turn up that he'd imagined he'd been there?

"Speech!" Darin called out from the front row. He grinned and led the audience into another round of applause.

Joel cleared his throat and waited for quiet. Everyone was

watching him, including the students behind him. "Thank you for coming this evening. This concert wouldn't have been possible without the hard work of so many people. Congratulations to our choir and orchestra." He turned to them. "It's been an honour to conduct you, and you'll be pleased to know there are no more rehearsals until next term, and as tomorrow is Saturday, you'll have the weekend to recover from tonight."

A couple of the students in the audience laughed, and some of the choir kids high-fived each other.

As he addressed the audience again, he took a deep breath. "I'm very happy to be a part of this school community. You're a huge part of my life, and… As I said earlier, conductors get nervous too. I nearly talked myself out of performing the Chopin for you this evening, but my partner convinced me I could do it. Working extra hours, and the stress that goes with that, isn't always good for a relationship, but he's always been there for me, as he is tonight." Joel caught Marcus's eye and smiled as their gazes met. Although most of the staff already knew he was gay, Joel couldn't go back from outing himself completely. He'd never thought of doing it before, but now he had a reason to. "Thank you, Marcus. I love you."

The audience all turned to see who Joel was looking at. Marcus's face was bright red, but he smiled and gave them a nod.

Two students—one from the orchestra and one from the choir—presented Joel with a tall paper bag decorated with music manuscript.

Joel thanked them, shook their hands, and gave the orchestra and choir a bow.

Adelaide took the microphone from him, but then put her hand over it so she wouldn't be heard. "Make your escape, Joel. You deserve it."

He opened his mouth to protest—there was clean-up to do, and he wasn't about to leave all of that to someone else.

"It's under control," Adelaide said as though she'd guessed what he was going to say. She grinned and indicated offstage. "Someone's waiting for you. Go enjoy that bottle of wine together before I change my mind."

Joel saw Marcus waiting in the wings. He must have snuck away during the presentation. "Thank you." Joel gave her a brief hug and made a hasty exit, not waiting to hear whatever she was going to say over the microphone.

Marcus already had Joel's coat and bag. He took Joel by the hand, and they made their escape before the students left the stage and noticed Joel was gone. When they reached the car, Marcus took Joel into his arms and kissed him.

"Congratulations on a job well done. You were amazing tonight." Marcus's smile was now a huge grin. "When you asked me if I minded if people knew we were together, I didn't expect you to announce it to the world like that. Wow."

"You don't mind, do you?" Although the question now sounded like an attempt to shut the barn door once the horse had bolted, Joel had to ask.

"Of course not." Marcus kissed Joel again. "You've made me very happy."

CHAPTER FIFTEEN

"I'm not going anywhere near work for at least the first week of these holidays." Joel lay stretched out on the sofa, with his feet on Marcus's lap. The concert had been an overwhelming success and raised more than the money they'd needed, even without the generous donation that had arrived anonymously a few days later.

Marcus raised an eyebrow. "Should I be looking for a pod and saving the real Joel from alien invaders?"

Joel tossed a cushion at him at the *Invasion of the Body Snatchers* reference. They'd watched the 1950s version of the movie the weekend before. Marcus hadn't seen a lot of older classic movies, so Joel decided it was something that needed rectifying, especially as Darin had a decent collection they could borrow.

"Don't worry, I'm still me." Joel took a sip of his coffee and let out a contented sigh. "No concert to worry about this break, so I can afford to take some time off. I do that occasionally, you know."

"Really?" Marcus laughed when Joel hunted for another cushion. They were heading down to Hokitika later in the week. Marcus was looking forward to their spending time with his parents who were excited by the opportunity to get to know Joel better.

The doorbell rang, and Marcus shoved Joel's feet off his lap. "I'll go answer that. You finish your coffee."

"Okay, thanks. Not going to argue with my brave monster hunter." Joel ignored Marcus's snort and swung his feet off the sofa so he could retrieve the book he'd dropped earlier.

Marcus held an envelope when he re-entered the room. "I found this taped to the front door." He handed it to Joel. "It's addressed to you, but I don't recognise the handwriting."

"I do," Joel said slowly. He ripped open the envelope, read through the letter inside quickly, and then scanned it again to make sure he hadn't misread the words.

"What is it?" Marcus asked, sitting down beside Joel. "Everything okay?"

"It's from Dad." Joel gave Marcus the letter. If someone else read it too, it meant the letter and its contents were real. "I... I thought I saw him at the concert, but when I looked again, he was gone."

"He was there," Marcus confirmed. "I saw him too. I figured it was a step forward, but when you didn't say anything, I thought you didn't want to talk about it. I wasn't going to push you." He grew quiet as he read the letter, then finally handed it back to Joel. "This is good, right? He wants to meet with you."

"Yeah, I guess." Joel hoped Marcus wasn't being overly optimistic. "If he wants to put things right, why leave the concert? He turned away when I tried to meet his gaze. And why skulk around leaving notes on our front door? He could have phoned me or posted a letter the way normal people do."

"Maybe he wanted to make sure you got it?" Marcus shuffled closer and put his arm around Joel. "He says in the letter he finds it difficult because of the number of years that have already passed."

"He's not the only one finding it difficult," Joel muttered. He dropped the letter onto his lap. "I don't know, Marcus. I thought… I…. After all this time, I should be happy he's finally contacted me, right? What if this is just to tell me to give up, and he's not interested? What if…?"

What if his father was angry because Joel had admitted he loved Marcus in front of everyone at the concert? Bad enough that Claude didn't accept his son's sexuality, but now everyone knew about it.

Joel sighed. His thoughts were bordering on ridiculous. Joel had been out for years and had never hidden who he was, although he hadn't advertised it either. No one had ever put two and two together and figured out he was related to the man who owned Ashcroft Engineering.

"Penny for them. I worry when you're quiet. It's never a good sign."

"I guess I'm scared of being hurt." Joel rested his head on Marcus's shoulder. "You'd think after all this time… I'm a grown man, and I know who I am. It's ridiculous. I don't need his approval."

"He's still your dad." Marcus reread the letter. "He wants to meet on neutral ground, so that's—"

"Yeah, right, and that makes the whole thing sound like we're getting ready for battle. I don't want to fight with him. I like my life right now, and I don't need him in it." Joel flinched.

"You don't really think that, do you?" Marcus kissed Joel's cheek. "It's okay to be scared. It's normal. You don't have to do this alone either. I can come with you, at least until he shows up, and then make my excuses and leave once you know everything is okay."

"I'd like that." Joel sighed again. "If I don't do this, I'll never know how it could have gone." As much as part of him wanted to run away from dealing with his dad, there wasn't really a choice. "At least he's let me choose the venue, even if he's specified the date and time."

"You're on holiday, he's not."

"Sometimes you're far too logical." Joel loved that Marcus could approach a situation calmly and sort through the details, while Joel often got bogged down by emotion if he thought about something for too long. He leaned over and grabbed his phone off the coffee table. "You can take the morning off?"

"Yeah, no problem. The weather's been good lately, so we've caught up quite a bit. I'll let Brendan know I'll be starting later."

"Okay. Thanks." Joel figured at least with it being the next morning, he wouldn't have to spend too much time thinking about it. Whatever his father wanted to say to him, he obviously wanted it over and done with as soon as he could. He brought up his father's name in his contacts list—Bernie had given him the number a while back. He typed a message and sent it.

A couple of minutes later, his phone told him he had a new message.

Thanks. See you then.

"I'm sure he'll be here soon." Marcus tried to sound positive for Joel's sake. "Perhaps he's not sure where the café is?"

"He brought me here years ago. He wouldn't have got lost." Joel shook his head when the waitress offered to top up his coffee.

"Thanks, none for me either. I've got quite a bit left."

Marcus glanced at the clock on the wall behind Joel. "Perhaps he's been held up at work."

"He would have texted." Joel sounded strained. "Dad's always been a stickler for punctuality, while Mum runs late. They used to drive each other crazy with it. I don't think he's coming, do you?"

"Why don't we give him another ten minutes?" Marcus suggested. He took a slow sip of his coffee. "This is a nice place, and I like the way they've converted the front of the house into a café yet left the rest intact. It fits in well with the houses on either side of it. I've never noticed it when I've driven past."

Despite the cooler weather, people sat outside at the tables and chairs on the deck, chatting in low tones while they finished their morning tea. The wooden fence out front gave the illusion of privacy, although the lattice work at the top of it was wide enough to see through. The painted sign hanging from the gate creaked back and forth in the breeze. Marcus would have offered to oil it, but no one else had commented on it.

"You're changing the subject." Joel shot him a glare, which Marcus didn't take personally.

"Yes, I am. You're nervous, and thinking about it isn't helping. I was trying to distract you." Marcus drained his coffee and placed his cup on the table.

They'd chosen an inside table tucked into a corner, which, despite giving them some privacy, also provided a good view of the ranch slider that was the café's front entrance.

"Thanks, but don't waste your time." Joel checked his phone again. "Still nothing. I guess he's not coming. So much for wanting to meet up with me." He shoved it back into his pocket. "Shit, how could I have been so stupid? He hasn't changed. Why the hell did I think one meeting could make everything right between us again?"

Marcus placed one hand over Joel's when Joel raised his voice. A woman at the next table glanced at them and then looked away again, clearly embarrassed by Joel's obvious distress.

"You're not stupid. I honestly think something's happened. Your dad might not approve of you being gay, but he wants you to be happy."

"Hah!" Joel picked up his cup, stared at it for a moment, and then slammed it down onto the table so hard that Marcus flinched. Joel grimaced and examined his cup. "Not broken. Thank God for one small mercy, at least. Sorry." He lowered his voice. "I'm so tired of all of this. I honestly thought this time might be different. I guess I wanted it to be different."

"Your father does want you to be happy." Marcus wanted so badly to make this better, to at least help Joel through his heartbreak. He hated seeing Joel so upset, but he didn't blame him. Although Marcus had made excuses for Claude, he couldn't understand why Claude would go to the trouble of setting this up and then not follow through. "He didn't strike me as—"

"As what?" Joel pulled his hand away. "I'm sorry and I know you're trying to help, but you haven't met him, and at this rate you're not likely to."

"Umm, well, actually…" Marcus cringed. The words had slipped out unintentionally. Now that they had, he wasn't going to lie to Joel. Keeping something from him wasn't the same.

"Well, actually?" Joel narrowed his eyes. "Please don't tell me what I think you're going to. You've met him, and you never told me?"

"Umm, yeah." Marcus reached for his cup, then remembered he'd already finished his coffee. "I was worried about you, and you wouldn't go see him, so when I said I could, and you said 'whatever'..."

"Whatever doesn't mean yes!" Joel glared at Marcus. "Fuck it. How dare you go see my father behind my back."

"I was worried about you," Marcus repeated. "So when you kind of agreed, I... I'm sorry, okay?" He deliberately softened his tone although he suspected it would be a waste of time. "He told me he wants you to be happy. That's all I wanted too."

Joel pushed back his chair. "You know how I feel about being with someone who plans stuff without telling me. I'm not some kid who needs protecting. I've got this, okay?" Joel's voice broke. "I've got this."

"Joel..." Marcus didn't know what else he could say. Perhaps he'd already said far too much.

"I... I'm sorry too." Joel stood and shoved his hands in his pocket. "I need some space. Please don't follow me. I need to think. About all of this."

He turned on his heel and stalked out of the café.

"Are you okay, sir?"

Marcus looked up to see the concerned waitress standing next to him. "I... I don't know." He couldn't go after Joel. Not now. No matter how much he wanted to. Yet he couldn't stay there either. He cleared his throat. "It's fine. Thanks for your concern, though. My... he's just got some bad news, that's all."

He didn't know why he felt the need to give an explanation to a stranger, but she nodded, smiled kindly at him, and went back to work.

Despite everything, Marcus couldn't switch off his need to protect Joel. Crap. How much had he screwed up? Joel would calm down, right?

Marcus felt sick, although he'd known what Joel's reaction would be. He mumbled a good morning to the barista as he paid for the coffee, and then he strode out of the café. Luckily, it was close to home, so they'd walked there. Marcus didn't think it was a good idea to drive right now.

He'd head home, pack a bag, and go around to Darin and Ella's. Joel had told him he needed some time to think things through. Marcus had screwed up by making the wrong move, so he'd back off and wait for Joel to make this one.

God, what if he didn't?

He had to, right? They'd argued before, and they would again. They'd talk things through and…

Damn it. Why hadn't Claude shown up? Marcus should have told Joel about seeing his dad weeks ago. But he'd been so nervous about the concert, and not sleeping anyway, and Marcus hadn't wanted to add to that.

Bloody hell. He was making excuses, and piss poor ones at that.

Sure, he'd done this with all the right intentions, but the damage was done. He had to hope Joel would forgive him and they could move forward.

Marcus picked up his pace, relieved yet disappointed when he reached home that Joel wasn't there. He choked back a sob, shoved a few clothes into his bag, left a scribbled note for Joel, and turned to leave.

Nannerl purred. He bent to pet her. "I'm sorry. Look after Joel for me. I'll be home soon."

He turned his keys over in his hand, started to remove Joel's house key, then hesitated. If he did that, he'd be admitting they were through. He wasn't ready to do that. Not yet.

He gripped them tightly, put them back in his pocket, and left, quietly shutting the front door behind him.

~

From across the road, Joel could hear the stream's song and see the double tree he always thought of as a symbol of love. Not thinking, he stepped out onto the road without looking. A car honked at him, and he darted back onto the pavement, his heart hammering.

The area by the stream was quiet, the storm clouds overhead adding to his state of mind. Joel strode over to the water, picked up a few sticks, and threw them into the stream. A few minutes later, he felt a little better, although his thoughts kept racing in a repetitive jumble.

Why would Dad set up this meeting, then not turn up?

Marcus had been trying to help. He loves me.

I need our relationship to be equal. I won't be with someone like Reed again.

Marcus and I are building something good together.

Aren't we?

Dad, where the hell are you? I want us to be the way we used to be so badly. Don't you?

Joel crouched by the water's edge, watching the current flow towards the footbridge. A drop of rain, then another, hit the water, sending slow ripples in his direction. He zipped up his jacket and retreated to stand under one of the larger trees. After finding a dry spot, he sat with his back to the trunk and tried to make sense of the morning.

He shoved his hands in his pockets, curling his fingers around the small case he'd collected from the jeweller the previous afternoon. He'd originally intended to talk to Marcus that evening, but he'd wanted to get their meeting at the café out of the way first. Asking Marcus to marry him was a huge step, and Joel hadn't wanted meeting up with his father to overshadow it.

Not that he had that problem now.

He'd reacted, rather than thought things through. Marcus's admission had touched on one of Joel's triggers. He still wasn't happy about what Marcus had done, but he shouldn't have sworn at him. Joel smiled despite his mood. Marcus had an overprotective streak a mile wide, and he'd only been trying to protect him, right?

Right.

A few months with Marcus were already so much better than the years he'd spent with Reed. Joel thought of the guilty expression Marcus had worn when he let it slip that he'd talked to Joel's dad. Not only guilt but concern and... fear?

Joel sighed. God, could he have screwed things up any more? So much for reacting like a mature adult and talking stuff through.

He stretched out his legs, ignoring the dampness from the grass seeping into his jeans. He'd sit and watch the rain for a bit, then head home and hope Marcus was there. They needed to talk, even if it was only to work out what they both wanted next.

His phone alerted him to the arrival of a text. He ignored it for a few minutes, then decided he'd better check it. What if something had happened to his dad?

Sorry, work came up. Try again tomorrow?

Joel snorted. So much for his dad making an effort. Marcus was wrong. Nothing had changed.

He punched in a reply and sent it.

Don't bother.

CHAPTER SIXTEEN

Joel picked up his phone, dialled Marcus's number, then hung up. God, he was a coward.

He'd hardly slept the last two weeks. They hadn't lived together for long, but Marcus had left more behind than a brief note. Joel tossed and turned all night, sitting bolt upright when he thought he heard Marcus's voice, only to remember he'd left.

Joel had said he needed some space. Marcus was respecting that. Right?

Nannerl whined from her spot by the front door. She'd taken to sitting there since Marcus had left, apart from sleeping on Marcus's side of the bed at night.

"Yeah, I know you miss him too." Joel smoothed out Marcus's note and read it through again.

I'm sorry. I still love you. Call me.

His phone rang. He answered it without checking the caller ID. "Marcus?"

A couple of moment later a familiar voice replied. "He's as miserable as you are. You know that, right?"

"Darin." Joel sighed. He put his phone on speaker and put

on the kettle to make coffee. "I thought you would have phoned before now to tell me what an idiot I've been."

"You're both idiots, and I would have, but Marcus didn't want me to." Darin sounded more resigned than angry. "He came and asked me whether he should talk to your dad. He was concerned about screwing things up between you but was more worried about doing nothing and then something happening to your dad."

"You *knew*?" Joel raised his voice. No wonder Darin had kept his distance the last few weeks too. "And you didn't tell me?"

"Think about it." Darin didn't alter his tone. "The guy is crazy about you, but he was prepared to lose you to do whatever it took to help you. The thing with your dad was eating you inside."

"*Is*," not was," Joel said slowly. "He wants me to call him, after all this?"

"Well, duh. He still loves you, but he's determined to give you your space because you asked him to." Darin sighed. "Bloody hell. Do I need to knock both your heads together? You're as stubborn as each other."

Ella called out in the background. "I'll help."

"Shit." Joel chewed on his bottom lip. "Is he there? Can I—"

"Nope, and I'm not doing this for you. You guys need to talk, and soon, okay? I think you're way past a phone call. Set up a meeting and talk to him."

"I'm sorry," Joel said softly. "Are we..." This was exactly why he and Marcus had hesitated about getting together.

"We're fine. I've known you long enough to know you'll eventually get your head out of your arse. We all make mistakes. Go fix yours." Darin hung up.

His phone rang again. This time Joel checked the ID, his hope dashing when it was only a call from his sister. He answered, annoyed, but knowing if he ignored her, she'd only keep calling until he answered. "Look, I don't know what Ella's told you but—"

Bernadette sounded frantic. "You need to meet me at the hospital. It's Dad. He's had another heart attack. Hillary phoned an ambulance for him at work. Mum's already there."

"Hospital?" Joel wobbled on his feet. He sagged into a nearby chair. "Oh fuck."

What if he'd left things too late? Why hadn't he taken up his dad's offer to try again to meet up?

He forced himself to focus. "Which hospital? I'm on my way." Joel took a deep breath and phoned Marcus's number again. This time he let it ring.

"Joel?" Marcus sounded hopeful, yet cautious.

"I'm sorry." Joel needed to get the words out before everything went to shit. If he lost his dad… he wouldn't be able to handle starting this conversation then, and Marcus had suffered enough. They both had. "Can we… can we talk." He grabbed his keys while he was talking and looked around for his coat. "Not now, but…"

"What's wrong?" Marcus got straight to the point.

"Dad. Hospital. I need… I just…"

"Are you at home?"

"Yeah, but—" Joel didn't have the right to ask for anything. Not after what he'd done.

"Do you want me there?"

"Yes." Joel blinked back tears. "But…"

"Stay put. You're not driving while you're upset. I'm close by. I'll take you."

Joel climbed into the SUV. He wouldn't meet Marcus's gaze. "I'm sorry."

"Yeah, you already said." Marcus pulled him into a brief hug. "I've missed you, but we can talk later, okay? You need to get to your dad. Focus on him now."

"Can you come in with me?" Joel glanced at Marcus. "I'm not sure I have the right, but... I need you."

Marcus backed out the driveway. "I still love you. That hasn't changed. I haven't stopped loving you. And you have every right to ask for anything you want. If you're sure you want me with you, I'll be there."

"Thanks." Joel leaned back in his seat and closed his eyes. Crap, he was crying. He scrubbed at his face quickly. "I still love you too."

They drove the rest of the way in silence, though Marcus took Joel's free hand in his and squeezed it. "There's not much parking at the hospital. I'll let you out and catch up with you at A&E. I'll be there as soon as I can."

Joel nodded, jumped out of the car as soon as Marcus pulled up, and ran for the emergency entrance of the hospital. The seats in the waiting room were full, and only a couple of people turned to look at him. He strode over to the receptionist.

"My father, Claude Ashcroft, was brought in by ambulance."

The woman gave him a sympathetic nod. "I'll check our records." After a few moments, she spoke to him again. "He's been taken through to a cubicle in the emergency ward. If you give me a few minutes, I'll see what I can find out for you. Who shall I say is inquiring?"

"Joel. Thank you."

She smiled at him kindly. "Take a seat, Joel. I won't be long."

He looked around for a seat but couldn't see a spare one. He preferred to stand anyway.

She'd spoken of his father as though he was still alive, so

that was a good sign, right? Not that she'd reveal much more than that without permission, and Joel doubted he was listed anywhere on Claude's records as family.

Where was Marcus?

Joel started to pace. Surely it couldn't take that long to find somewhere to park. He didn't want to do this alone. To hear that his father was—

He cut off that thought. Not going there. Not until he had to. How long was not too long? He glanced at his watch.

"Why don't you sit down? You're using a lot of energy there, young man." An older lady spoke to him softly and gestured for the boy with her to give up his seat. "They're very busy here today, so if she's taking a while, it's probably why. We've already been here for an hour."

Joel managed a shaky smile. "Thanks, but I'll be fine." The boy with her looked familiar, and he seemed to know who Joel was too, although he was too young to be a student at the high school.

The boy tugged at the old lady's sleeve. He had a bandage on one arm and winced when he moved it. "That's Mr Ashcroft, Nana. He's the music teacher at Austin's school. Remember the concert we went to?"

She peered at him more closely. "Why so it is, Barry. It's lovely to see you again, Mr Ashcroft, but I wish it was in better circumstances. I overheard you tell the receptionist that your father had been brought in. I hope it's nothing too serious."

"Thanks." Joel figured out why the boy seemed familiar. "You're Austin West's brother, aren't you?" Austin played trombone in the orchestra.

"Yeah. I fell off my skateboard and hurt my arm." Barry looked up when the doors to the entrance slid open. "Isn't that your partner? I remember you introduced him at the concert."

Joel followed Barry's gaze, and relief flooded through him. "Yes. And thanks." He waved Marcus over as the receptionist called Joel's name.

Marcus caught up with Joel in time to hear the news.

"Sorry for the wait," the receptionist said. "I've spoken to the nurse and to your mother and sister. Your father is stable, and he's been asking for you." She peered past Joel to Marcus. "I'm sorry but only one of you can go in."

"I'll be here when you get back," Marcus said quickly. "However long it takes."

"Thanks." Joel waited for the receptionist to open the door to let him in. He heard Barry introduce himself to Marcus before the door closed behind them.

The receptionist led him through a corridor to a cubicle in the corner. "Hello, Mr Ashcroft. Joel's here to see you."

Bernadette and Jill sat on opposite sides on the bed. Jill held Claude's hand, although he seemed to be asleep. When she saw Joel, she immediately stood and hugged him.

"Oh, Joel. I'm so pleased you're here."

Claude lay on a hospital bed, his chest rising and falling in a regular rhythm. He had leads attached to his chest, and one finger enclosed in a plastic clip to register his heart rate. He wasn't wearing an oxygen mask. Joel was hopeful that was a good sign, although a closer look revealed an oxygen line hooked under his nose.

"Hillary noticed how pale and unwell he looked," Bernadette said quietly. "She gave him an aspirin and phoned for the ambulance immediately. The doctor said he'd had a heart attack." She hugged Joel once Jill finally let go of him. "When I got the call, I panicked. I thought it was a lot worse. I hope I didn't scare you."

"There's no point in feeling guilty," Jill said briskly. "You're both here, and that's the important thing. Now pull up that spare chair for your brother. Your father will want to know he's here when he wakes up."

"He's been asking for you," Bernadette said. "Saying your name over and over. The nurse finally convinced him to try and sleep."

"We were supposed to meet for morning tea a couple of weeks ago, but he cancelled… said it was because of work." Joel leaned over his father, brushed his hair back from his face, and then took Claude's hand in his. Joel had always thought of his father as a strong man. Seeing him in a hospital bed and looking so pale scared him. "He tried to reschedule, but I…." He swallowed, trying to stop the tears.

God, he hadn't given his father a chance. Claude had tried to make another time to meet up, something he'd never done before, even when Joel was a child. If work called, whatever they'd had planned was forfeit.

"Joel." Claude opened his eyes and whispered Joel's name again. His fingers curled around his son's. "I'm sorry. I wanted to see you again, and then when this happened… I thought I'd left it too late."

"Dad," Joel said in a choked voice. "It's fine. I… I'm so pleased you're…." *Okay* didn't seem the right word, given the circumstances.

"The doctor said he's very lucky," Jill said. "They're going to move him up to the Coronary Care Unit as soon as they can organise a bed. He'll need to do more than take medication and whatever other treatment they decide on. This was a warning to make some changes in his life, and one he is going to take notice of."

Claude winced but nodded meekly. Joel had never seen him react that way to something Jill had said before.

Jill exchanged a glance with Bernadette. "We're going to make ourselves a cup of tea so you men can talk. Would you like one, Joel?"

"Thanks, Mum." Joel hoped she knew he wasn't only thanking her for the tea.

Bernadette gave Joel another hug and then followed their mother down the corridor.

"This isn't the way I pictured us meeting up again," Claude said finally. "I would have preferred a nice quiet cup of tea in that café I used to take you to."

"I thought the worst when Bernie called me." Joel squeezed his father's hand. "I thought I'd left it too late, too. I didn't... I know we don't agree on... you know... but I still love you. You're still my dad."

Claude's lips curved up into a shaky smile. "And you're still my son. I told your young man that I want you to be happy." He grew silent.

Joel heard the *but* that hung in the air between them. "You still don't accept who I am, do you?" he asked slowly.

"I've missed you, and this has shown me that life isn't always as long as we'd like it to be." Claude admitted. "I should have tried to contact you years ago. And I shouldn't have made the mistake of taking no for an answer when you put me off a couple of weeks ago—although I can understand why you did. I said some horrible things to you all those years ago, and the longer I left it, the harder it was to try to tell you I was sorry."

"You told me I was a disappointment." Joel bit his lip. Now wasn't the time to be having that conversation.

"And a few other things I shouldn't have said." Claude closed his eyes for a moment, then met Joel's gaze. "I might not always agree with how you live your life." He held up a hand to stop Joel interrupting. "I've been brought up to think a certain way, and it's not easy to push that aside, but I want to try. I'd like us to be at least on speaking terms."

"I'd like that too." Joel hadn't thought he'd get even that from Claude. When he thought about how he might not see… It would be enough. It had to be. But if Claude wanted Joel in his life, he'd have to accept his relationship with Marcus too, and keep his opinions to himself.

"You're thinking, son. I can hear it from here." Claude teased Joel like he used to years ago.

"Being gay isn't a choice, and I need to live my live honestly and be who I am. I love Marcus, and he's important to me. Whatever your issues with me, I don't want you to include him in that."

"I can't promise you what I think you want to hear, but I can promise to keep my opinions to myself, at least in front of him. I'm trying. Nothing will make a man rethink his priorities like believing you've left the important things too late."

"Definitely." Joel fidgeted with the hem of his shirt. He was all too aware he'd been heading down that road with Marcus too. "I guess we're more alike in some ways than I wanted to admit."

"If you want something or someone you have to grab it with both hands and hang on to it." Claude looked sheepish. "I used to tell you that when you were a child. It's time I followed my own advice." He smiled. "Marcus loves you too. It would have taken a lot for him to come talk to me. Remember that." He cleared his throat. "One step at time for us, and if we take a couple back, we try again. Is that okay with you?"

"Yes." Joel smiled. "That's very okay with me."

Marcus expected Joel to be quiet on the way home from the hospital, so he wasn't surprised when Joel didn't initiate conversation. He'd waited for over an hour for Joel to return to the waiting room. Hopefully it was a good sign that Joel and his father had finally said what needed saying—or at least made a step in that direction.

However, Joel and his dad weren't the only ones who needed to talk.

"Do you want to come in?" Joel asked when they pulled up outside the house.

"Yes, but..." Marcus hesitated. "You have a lot to think about, and I understand if you—"

After what Joel had been through with Claude, another twenty-four hours wouldn't hurt. "We need to talk, and this is your home too." Joel caressed Marcus's cheek, then hesitated. "If you still want it to be."

"I do. Very much so." Marcus leaned into Joel's touch and placed his hand over Joel's. "I've missed you. Being apart has made me realise how much better my life is with you in it."

"That's how I feel about you." Joel opened the front door and quickly stepped out of Nannerl's way when she headed straight for Marcus and headbutted him. "She's been waiting by the front door for you ever since you left. And she's been shedding like crazy on your side of the bed too."

Marcus bent to pat her. "I've missed you too." He smiled when she wound her tail around his legs. "You'll need to be patient, though. Your dad and I need to talk."

"She's not the only one who's happy you're home." Joel kissed Marcus briefly on the cheek. "I could do with some tea. I'll make some and meet you in the living room."

Joel took a while making the tea. Marcus suspected he'd given him too much space over the past two weeks, but he still waited on the sofa. Nannerl spread herself across his lap. He eased her onto the floor when Joel entered the room. She made herself comfortable on the other sofa, one eye watching both of them.

"I'm glad your dad is going to be okay." Marcus finally broke the awkward silence.

"Yeah, me too." Joel put his tea down and took Marcus's hand in his. "I'm sorry we argued. I might not have liked what you did, but I know you meant well."

"I'm sorry too." Marcus met Joel's gaze. His eyes seemed dimmer than usual, although Marcus figured that was probably because of his own guilty conscience. "I shouldn't have gone to see your father. I was worried about you, and I grabbed a very slim thread to convince myself you'd said it was okay to talk to him, when deep down I knew you hadn't."

"When I said whatever, I didn't mean yes or whatever you want," Joel said softly. "But I shouldn't have reacted the way I did either. You acted out of concern and because you love me. I can't stay angry at you for that."

"Yes, I did." Marcus bit his lip. "I know this isn't an excuse, but I'm not Reed. I don't want to make your decisions for you. You don't need to be with someone who does that. I want an equal relationship, one in which we discuss everything."

Joel raised an eyebrow.

"However," Marcus added, "I'm not perfect either, and I make mistakes. This was a big one."

"Given what happened with Dad today, I think it was the right call. I make mistakes too. Taking off in a huff isn't the mature way to deal with this kind of crap. And when Dad texted to arrange a different time, I told him not to bother." He cringed, then picked up his tea and took a long sip of it. "Dad said you talked to him. Whatever you said to him, I think it made our conversation go easier. So, thank you. But don't do it again, okay?"

"Okay."

Marcus studied Joel for a moment. He had curled his legs under him and was cradling the hot cup like it was something precious.

"How did the conversation with your dad go? If you don't want to tell me, that's fine. I know it's private."

"The other thing I want from a relationship is to be able to share everything." Joel studied his cup again. "He said he wanted me to be happy, but he doesn't agree with the way I've chosen to live my life."

"I'm sorry." Marcus had hoped Claude would come around, that his latest health scare might make him realise he'd screwed up.

"He apologised for what he said to me all those years ago." Joel traced the moisture collecting on the rim of his cup with one finger. "He does want to try, so that's huge." His breath hitched, and he wiped at his eyes. "Damn it. Is it so wrong that I want things between Dad and I to be like they used to be?"

"It's not wrong." Marcus gently prised the cup from Joel's fingers and placed both their cups on the coffee table. He took Joel into his arms and held him. "Trying is good, though, right? And you guys have a lot of years to make up for. Get to know each other again first. One step at a time."

Joel let out a sob. "That's what he said. One step at a time." He buried his head on Marcus's shoulder.

"It's okay. I'm here." Marcus kissed Joel's hair. "I love you. We'll get through this together. I promise."

"Thanks." Joel glanced up at Marcus.

Marcus caught a tear with his finger.

"I meant what I said when I told you I still love you," Joel said. "Thanks for being here for me and putting up with all my crap."

"Yeah," Marcus said. "I meant it when I told you that too." He smiled and cupped Joel's chin. "We all have our own crap, and this is what relationships are about. If life was perfect, it would be kind of boring."

"I guess." Joel leaned into Marcus's touch. "Just be with me?"

"Of course. Whatever you need, whenever you need it, if I can be here for you, I will be. I promise."

Joel smiled and spoke slowly. "Dad told me something else today. He said if I want something I should go for it, grab it with both hands, and hang on to it."

"Good advice." Marcus frowned when Joel grabbed both of Marcus's hands. "Huh, what?"

"He meant you," Joel said softly, "and I intend to do just that."

~

Joel pulled up near the spot by the stream he'd first taken Marcus to nearly four months earlier. He slipped his hand into his pocket and smiled.

Two months had passed since that awful day at the hospital. Although Joel had no doubts about his feelings for Marcus, he'd wanted to wait to make sure they still *both* wanted a future together.

In some ways, it felt as though Marcus had never left, but little things *had* changed in their life together. Joel made a point, now, of taking Sundays off no matter how big his workload; apart from doing "couple things," they'd spent a lot of time talking about what they wanted in their relationship. Claude's health issues had made Joel reassess his own tendency to take on too much, although he slipped on occasion. When he did, Marcus raised an eyebrow and gently reminded Joel about his promise to take care of himself.

They resolved arguments or came to a compromise as soon as they could, and despite a couple of blips they were working hard at being completely open with each other.

"Why are we here? Should I worry?"

Joel chuckled. "Definitely not." He caught Marcus's lips in a kiss, then opened the car door. He waited until Marcus joined him by the curb, then led him by the hand to the tree with the split trunk. "You trust me, right?"

"Of course." Marcus blew out white breaths of air. "Although I'm not sure why we're doing this at night. It's freezing."

"We were both working today, and I wanted to do this today, on the two-month anniversary of us moving back in together."

Despite the cold, it was a clear night, and the area was illuminated by moonlight and the pale glow of nearby streetlights.

Marcus frowned. "Whatever you want to talk about, we could have done it at home."

"Ssh, I wanted this to be romantic and you're ruining the mood." Joel wanted to do this here, at a place that held memories for both of them. With Marcus's love of nature, it doubly felt like the right spot.

He got down on one knee and fished a small jeweller's box out of his pocket. "I love you, Marcus, with everything I am. Will you marry me?"

Marcus opened his mouth as though he was about to speak, but nothing came out.

"Marcus?" *Oh God.* Had he done the wrong thing? What if Marcus said no? What if—

"Yes, yes, yes! Oh, God, yes. I love you. Of course I'll marry you!" Marcus flushed. "I'd bought a ring when we went to see my parents in Hokitika last month, but I hadn't found the right moment to ask you. This is totally it," he added quickly, "although I was planning to bring you here tomorrow and ask you. In daylight, when it's not so bloody cold out."

Joel laughed. "We can totally repeat this tomorrow if

you'd like, although you already know what my answer is. Yes, totally yes."

"We don't need to come back tomorrow, unless you want to." Marcus grinned. "Aren't you forgetting something?"

Joel looked at him blankly, then clicked. "Oh yeah." He pulled the case from his pocket, and opened it, then slipped the ring on Marcus's finger. "I was going to ask you that day we were going to meet my dad," he said softly.

"No regrets." Marcus wiped a tear from Joel's cheek. He looked close to tears too. "We're going to have an amazing future together. That's what matters."

EPILOGUE

"Honestly, Marcus, give it here." Ella attached the floral spray to Marcus's lapel and then stood back to admire her handiwork. "You make a very handsome groom."

"Thanks." Marcus didn't get why she'd insisted he and Joel get ready in separate rooms. They'd already ditched tradition by spending the night before together and had been sharing Joel's—their—house for months.

"I'm your best woman. Let me do my job." Ella fished her camera from her handbag and took a photo. Although they'd hired a professional photographer, she'd insisted on taking some personal shots. Once she'd embarrassed Marcus even more, she patted the sofa and waited for him to sit next to her.

Joel and Marcus had decided on a small wedding with just family and a few close friends. They'd looked at a few different venues, but when Ella and Darin offered their garden and house for the wedding and reception, they'd realised the perfect place had been right in front of them the whole time. Marcus had spent the last few months getting the section into shape, and it looked great.

"Thanks for everything." Marcus kissed his sister on the cheek. "We really appreciate it."

"We're family, and we're really excited to welcome Joel into the family for real." Ella smiled. "He's been an honorary member for years, and I always figured you two would be good together, even if it took you both longer than anyone else to figure that out."

"It takes some of us longer than others," Marcus teased her. "Thanks for playing matchmaker. We love you for it."

Although Ella claimed Darin and Isabel had been the main culprits in what Isabel now called *Operation Matchmaker*, Marcus knew his sister well enough to be certain she'd probably masterminded the whole thing.

"Everyone decent in there?" Clifford Verden poked his head around the partly open door.

"Sure, Dad. Mum, you can come in too," Marcus said. If his father was out there, his mother wouldn't be far behind.

"You look lovely." Glenda Verden kissed her son on the cheek. "So handsome." She dabbed at her eyes with her handkerchief. She'd cried at Ella's wedding too. "We've just chatted to Joel. I'm sure you two will be very happy together. You're good for each other, you know. A mother can tell."

"Thanks, Mum." Marcus grinned.

His mother had said that to him every time he and Joel had seen them since the first trip they'd made together to Hokitika, shortly after Claude was released from hospital.

Joel and his father had spent the past nine months working towards mending their relationship. Claude had also admitted he'd donated to the fundraiser and stepped up to take over the sponsorship the school had lost. Joel had been hesitant to take up his offer; he didn't want to owe his father anything. But Claude had insisted he was doing it for the kids, having seen the difference music had made in Joel's life at that age. He'd also reassured Joel and the PTA that his support had nothing to do with his relationship with his son. He'd been looking for a way to give back to his community for a while, and this was the perfect opportunity.

Marcus stood, anxious to get his wedding started, but Glenda smiled and laid a hand on his arm, stopping him.

"Almost time," she said, "but I wanted one last word with both of you." She chuckled. "I've never seen Isabel so excited. It was a great idea asking her to be the ring bearer. She's done nothing but gush about how her two favourite uncles are finally getting married."

"We're her only uncles," Marcus pointed out. Given Isabel's determination to get him and Joel together, it was only right that she take a role in the ceremony.

Ella elbowed him.

Clifford grinned. "Come on, Glenda. Your daughter has that look just like the one you get. I say we head somewhere safely out of range and take our seats."

"Coming." Glenda rolled her eyes. "We love you, Marcus, and we're so proud."

Joel peered out the window again. "Damn it," he muttered.

"He wished you and Marcus well," Darin reminded him. "That's a huge step for your dad, and he's still got plenty of time if he decides to come."

"Dad's always on time for everything." Joel sighed. "If he wanted to be here, he would be by now."

Nannerl rubbed up against his legs in a final attempt to shed over his trousers. He bent to pet her, and she purred loudly. She'd stayed inside, away from most of their visitors, and spent the majority of the day demanding attention from either Joel or Marcus, until Isabel had distracted her with a piece of string. She'd moved into Darin and Ella's a few days earlier so she'd be used to being there while Joel and Marcus were away on their honeymoon.

"Everything's all set." Bernadette ducked back into the room. "All we need now is a couple of grooms and we're ready to go."

"Thanks for everything, Bernie." Joel gave his sister a hug. She and Ella had worked hard to pull everything together. Despite the wedding being a small affair, there had still been a lot to organise. Their day would be exactly the way they wanted it, but neither of their sisters had let Joel or Marcus do any of the work.

"It's not every day I get to see my brother get married, so having you too exhausted to enjoy it wouldn't do at all." Bernadette grinned. "Ella and I make a great team." She looked thoughtful. "I see more collaboration in our future."

Darin groaned.

"Great!" Joel tried to sound enthusiastic to distract Bernadette from Darin's reaction. While he appreciated everything they'd done, he'd found it difficult to stand aside and let them take over.

"Gee, thanks." Bernadette chuckled and kissed Joel on the cheek. "Don't be so nervous. This day will be great, and Marcus is crazy about you. He's a lucky guy."

"I'm the lucky one," Joel murmured. He adjusted his tie yet again, then ran his fingers through his hair.

The weather had decided to cooperate, so they hadn't had to settle for the living room—aka plan B—although it was plenty big enough.

He and Darin followed Bernadette out the French doors, letting her go ahead so she could take her seat with the rest of her family. Her husband, Keith, had looked after their boys for the morning. He'd given Joel an uncharacteristic hug when he'd arrived. Keith had never been one for showing his emotions, but he and Joel had grown closer since Joel's return to the regular Sunday family lunches he'd missed for so long. Keith and Marcus had become good friends too.

"All set?" Marcus asked quietly from behind Joel, making him jump.

"Yeah." Joel turned to look at his soon-to-be husband, and his mouth felt suddenly dry. Marcus wore a dark suit, his tie a lighter grey that matched his eyes. "Wow. You look great."

Marcus flushed. "You clean up well yourself." Joel's suit was the same colour, but his tie was blue.

Darin stepped in between them. "Behave yourselves until you're married." He linked his arm through Ella's and let out a low whistle. "I need to take you to more weddings, sweetheart." He leaned in to kiss her.

Joel coughed loudly. "Behave *yourselves*."

"Adults." Isabel came up behind her father and rolled her eyes.

The opening bars of the Chopin nocturne Joel and Marcus had chosen filled the garden. Joel slipped his hand into Marcus's, and they walked up the aisle between their guests to the wedding celebrant. Toni gave them a smile as they passed her at the keyboard, yet she didn't falter as she continued to play.

Isabel followed her uncles, with Ella and Darin behind her.

"Welcome to the wedding of Joel and Marcus." Belinda, the marriage celebrant, smiled warmly. "I'm delighted to be here. However, I know it's not me you're here to see, so…"

Ella leaned across and whispered something in Belinda's ear.

Joel frowned and glanced at Marcus, who shrugged.

"Before we go further, there is someone here who wants to speak before Joel and Marcus exchange their vows." Belinda gestured to the side door. "Please come forward."

Joel turned to see Claude walking towards them. Joel's

breath hitched, and a chill crept up his spine. Surely his father wasn't going to make a scene.

Marcus took Joel's hand in his and squeezed it.

Claude gave both of them a nod as he approached. "I'm not good at public speaking, but this is something I should have said a long time ago." He cleared his throat. "Joel and I haven't always seen eye to eye on everything, and we were estranged for far too long. I can't take back everything I've said to him, but I am sorry for so much of it. I love my son, and I wish him and Marcus a very happy life together. I'm not losing a son today, but gaining another."

"Oh, Dad," Joel whispered. "Thank you. I love you too." He started to wipe his tears, but Marcus leaned over and brushed them away gently.

"Thank you, Claude," he said softly. "This means a lot to both of us."

Claude ducked his head the same way Joel did when he was embarrassed. "Make your old man proud," he told Joel and then took his seat next to Jill.

Isabel handed Marcus's ring to Joel. It was plain gold on the outside, but with a leaf pattern engraved on the inside, a reminder of Marcus's love of nature and how much he enjoyed working with it.

"I, Joel Andrew Ashcroft, take you, Marcus Nicholas Verden, as my husband." Joel slipped the ring he held onto Marcus's finger—he'd told Joel when he'd taken it off that morning his hand had felt bare without it. "This ring is a symbol of my love for you. You complete me, and I know you'll always be there for me whenever I need you. I trust you with my heart, my life, and my future."

Marcus took Joel's ring from Isabel. He'd added an engraving to it, as Joel had to the ring he'd given Marcus— tiny musical symbols.

"I, Marcus Nicholas Verden, take you, Joel Andrew Ashcroft, as my husband."

Marcus returned Joel's ring to his finger. Joel had told him he'd felt its absence for the few hours he'd been without it.

"This ring," Marcus said, "is a symbol of my love for you. You complete me, and I know you'll always be there for me whenever I need you. I trust you with my heart, my life, and my future."

"I now pronounce you husbands," Belinda said. "Congratulations!"

As they leaned in for their first kiss as a married couple, a pair of tuis flew overhead, landing in a nearby kowhai tree, their unique song filling the air.

Joel smiled when he broke the kiss. "Chopin provided the prelude to our first kiss, and nature joined in for our first as a married couple."

Marcus brushed his lips against Joel's again. He placed his left hand next to Joel's, and the sunlight caught their rings.

A violin and flute joined the keyboard in welcoming them to their future together, adding their music to that of the tuis.

"I love you," Joel murmured. "You've made me very happy."

He leaned in to capture another kiss. One by one the instruments faded away until only the keyboard was left playing the prelude they both knew so well.

Marcus smiled. "Our prelude," he whispered, "my love."

ABOUT THE AUTHOR

CONNECT WITH ANNE
Contact me at:
annebarwell.wordpress.com
darthanne@gmail.com

Anne Barwell lives in Wellington, New Zealand. She shares her home with Kaylee: a cat with "tortitude" who is convinced that the house is run to suit her; this is an ongoing "discussion," and to date, it appears as though Kaylee may be winning.

In 2008, Anne completed her conjoint BA in English Literature and Music/Bachelor of Teaching. She has worked as a music teacher, a primary school teacher, and now works in a library. She is a member of the Upper Hutt Science Fiction Club and plays violin for Hutt Valley Orchestra.

She is an avid reader across a wide range of genres and a watcher of far too many TV series and movies, although it can be argued that there is no such thing as "too many." These, of course, are best enjoyed with a decent cup of tea and further the continuing argument that the concept of "spare time" is really just a myth. She also hosts and reviews for other authors, and writes monthly blog posts for Love Bytes. She is the co-founder of the New Zealand Rainbow Romance writers, and a member of RWNZ.

Anne's books have received honourable mentions five

times, reached the finals four times—one of which was for best gay book—and been a runner up in the Rainbow Awards. She has also been nominated three times in the Goodreads M/M Romance Reader's Choice Awards—twice for Best Fantasy, once for Best Historical, and once for All-Time Favourite M/M Author.